DEREK HEATH

DEAD ENGINES

STORIES

POPE LICK PRESS

2024

CONTENTS

INTRODUCTION

A quick note before you board:

Inside this book, you will find six tales of a considerably niche subgenre of horror, though one that has existed for a very long time. Dickens' nineteenth-century *The Signal-Man* is just one of many classic horror stories that traverse the railway, others including Rosemary Timperley's *The Underground People*, W.G. Kelly's *A Smoking Ghost*, and (my personal favourite of recent memory) the haunting *Railhead* by Perceval Landon.

I do not hope, in printing these stories, to come anywhere close to the atmosphere or talent that these stories – and so many others like them – displayed. Nor do I hope to emulate those classics with a knowledge of the railway to any similar degree as that clearly possessed by the authors. I am almost concerned, indeed, that a collection of stories with such a narrow theme might become tedious to any readers used to my usual creature features.

So why the railway?

In truth, I have always felt that there was something inherently frightening about riding a train. On my mother's side, my family is connected deeply to the railway, and though I have not ridden a train myself for some time I remember the feeling well: the rattle of the wheels; the thundering of the earth beneath you; the constant hammering of the floor…

There is something out there on the rails, and with these few stories I hope to explore what that might be.

So I do hope you like them. We begin with a collision, then move into more bloodthirsty territory, before delving into cosmic and haunting horrors alike…

Tickets, if you will.

Enjoy the ride!

Derek Heath

August 2023

THE FATE OF THE CIRCADIA

Hamish stared blankly out of the bedroom window, his tired eyes searching the farmland below. The sloping hill was splashed with the faint grey of dawn sunlight as it split violently on the horizon; there was birdsong, and the distant call of the rooster.

No sign of them yet.

Behind him in the bed, Jason was stirring. "Again?" he groaned, fumbling for Hamish in the half-light before clocking the big, broad-shouldered figure in the windowframe. "Honestly, my love, you don't have to keep doing this."

Hamish turned, buttoning his shirt with thick fingers. The muscles of his arms and neck strained against the flannel, the barrel of his chest trembling with every faintly-asthmatic wheeze. His beard had grown thick and black, his hair a mess of oily tangles. Squinting across the room at

9

him, Jason could tell he'd been up for a while already.

"Please, come back to bed."

"I can't," Hamish said. Outside the rooster shrieked again, its cry booming. The smell of manure drifted up from the farm, seeping through the single-glazing. "I'm sorry. I'll be back up soon."

"No, you won't," Jason smiled thinly. "Once you've done this, you'll get to work with the cows."

Hamish paused. "Yeah," he said eventually, his voice low and quiet.

"Fine," Jason said, flopping back into the bed. "Go do what you've got to do. I'm having a lie-in."

Silently, Hamish pulled up his corduroys and glanced again at the window. He grabbed the newspaper from the sill before crossing the sill, boards creaking under his heavy footsteps.

"Of all the things your father could've left you," Jason muttered. "You'd think the farm was enough."

Hamish froze in the doorway. Recent memories stirred horribly, upsettingly, inside him. "I have to do it," he whispered.

"Sure," Jason said, sitting up again and staring at his husband's back. "Just like your dad had to do it, and his dad before him… I get it, Hamie."

"I'm sorry."

"Don't be," Jason shrugged. "Just remember… the line stops here. When you're gone – when *we're* gone – they're on their own. You understand that, don't you? You can't do this for them forever."

"Yeah. I know."

Hamish stumbled onto the landing and trotted calmly down the stairs, his head pounding with guilt.

Faint traces of sunlight began to bristle on the carriage windows, highlighting the dust and soot that had gathered on the rattling glass.

Nina had chosen a seat in the sleeper car but had found herself too eager to drift off, instead enjoying the quiet rumbling of the train as they crossed the darkened English countryside. She sketched as she rode, her pad open in her lap, a set of charcoal pencils tucked into a paper bag beside her. She had a bacon sandwich in her bag for breakfast but dawn was still a good few minutes away and she had another three or four hours left on the train; she was hoping to hold off until seven or eight in the morning, at least, though that optimism was being slowly diminished by the gradually-increasing cramps in her stomach.

Closing her sketchbook, Nina drew a deep breath and gazed out of the window.

The country rolled past as the *Circadia* burrowed between two shallow hills. Bent, gnarly trunks exploded out of the hillsides, thick knots of root worming in and out of the grass. The treetops were dashed with red and gold and waved gently in the wind. Either side of the tracks, the earth was scorched dry and black and splattered with gravel. The sky crackled and swam above, banks of cloud tinted with syrupy light.

This was the best day of Nina's life.

She had accepted the position largely out of a desire to move from the city and lead a somewhat quieter life; she had been pleasantly surprised, however, to discover that the role was offering about twenty pounds a week more than she'd expected, and that she would be provided with accommodation on the estate. She couldn't believe at first that she'd been selected for the job but now she was on her way and it couldn't be more real. It was happening. She could be earning twice as much by 1950 if she proved good enough, and in the meantime she'd be able to send a good portion of her wage back home to her mother. She smiled to herself as the carriage rocked beneath her.

Today was the day everything changed.

Across from her, a young woman slept quietly in the folds of a great grey overcoat, her husband looking sternly out of the window beside her. The woman's head rested gently on his shoulder; Nina wondered where they were going, whether they were happy. There was snoring behind her and had been for the past hour, and occasionally she would glimpse the sleeping bald-headed man's reflection in her window when a splash of darkness hit the glass. There might have been a dozen people in the sleeper carriage; perhaps four times as many upon the *Circadia* altogether. The train was famous for its punctuality and the way in which it had performed the same six-hour journey every single day since before the turn of the century; never once had it been late (except for a brief period between

1915 and 1916 where a good stretch of the rails had been destroyed; the *Circadia* had resumed its usual services no more than twenty-four hours after the line was fully repaired).

Punctual was good.

Punctual showed just how desperately Nina needed this job.

A thin wisp of sooty steam danced past the window and Nina returned to her sketchbook. The train barrelled around a curve, splashes of green whipping past as the rails careened gently off to the right. There was something genuinely comforting about the whirr of the pistons, about the consistent chuffing rhythm of the carriage. She drew something dreamlike and vaguely incomprehensible, taking inspiration not from anything specific but from the warm pulse of emotions inside her. Outside streaks of colour washed onto the glass and washed away again. Her stomach had settled. Nina shifted in her seat, folding one leg over the other, and closed her eyes. Content, she smiled softly to herself.

The long, bellowing blast of the train's horn detonated around her and she bolted out of her reverie, eyes immediately moving to the front of the carriage. The horn sounded a second time, a scream of sound that seemed to break the countryside apart. Around her those who had been sleeping began to stir awake, confusion rippling from one to the other.

Nina's stomach twisted into a tight knot as another sound joined the blare of the horn: the frantic ringing of a brass bell, passing from carriage to carriage. Some kind of alarm.

Something was wrong.

As the horn sounded for a third time Nina looked out of the window. She clutched the sketchbook in one hand, not realising that her knuckles were bulging white against the flesh. Her legs had clamped together and anxiety pounded the inside of her chest. The bell was still ringing and she could only imagine some poor panicked soul tugging on the rope to sound it at the front of the train—

She saw it.

The *Circadia* was still cruising around a bend in the rails and looking out through the window she could see the track before them: there was another train rocketing toward them.

"Oh, dear god," she whispered. The train was a

colossus of black steel spewing fumes into the sky, coming down the rails at a speed she couldn't comprehend. She heard the screaming of metal on metal and knew that the driver of the oncoming train was trying to brake – but it was no good – the train was hardly slowing, and the distance between the two locomotives was closing at an alarming rate with every passing second.

Someone behind her screamed, but she hardly noticed. She was staring at the train, her gaze locked onto the mechanical beast as it screamed closer and closer. There was something wrong with it.

There was something wrong with the train.

"What…" she whispered, laying her hand against the glass. It took her a moment to discern just what it was about the train that unsettled her so badly – aside from the fact they were seconds away from colliding headlong with it – but then she realised, and her blood went cold. The glass rattled against the palms of her fingers. The countryside streaked past, no slower than before.

The oncoming train flickered in and out of existence, its shape blurring and clarifying before her eyes. Closer. The lamps burned red, the windows filled with flickering amber light; the train seemed to buzz and bend, twisting in and out of itself multiple times a second. In one frantic fraction of a second she saw it, as real and solid as anything, and then for the next it wasn't there at all. Closer. Bolts of steel seemed to thrust out of the engine and whip back into themselves, the carriages blurring manically in a miasma of black and red. *Closer—*

The train kissed the *Circadia* on the mouth.

The oncoming train scythed remorselessly into the *Circadia*, the two engines crumpling in a detonation of mangled metal and fire. Steam exploded into the valley and rolled up the hillsides as two snakes of steel and iron jounced off the rails, screaming past each other with a horrific scraping, crashing, booming sound.

All the windows in the sleeper car shattered at once, glass flying everywhere. A shower of tiny pieces skirted Nina's cheek, drawing tiny beads of blood. She gasped as her head thumped into the back of the seat before her. The other passengers screamed as they were thrown about the carriage, sparks flying off the rails and blotting out the behemoth of coal-fired death that roared deafeningly past them in a blossom of electric points.

Then the carriage was tipped onto its roof as the *Circadia* twisted horribly into the hillside, corkscrewing over itself. Behind them – before them; all around them – the other train was separating, hunks of it flying into the valley. Something caught ablaze and Nina felt a great *whoof* of heat sear the inside of the sleeper car.

Everything went black.

When she awoke, the world around her was smoking.

Her chest exploded in a fit of coughing as she tried to move, a haze of black soot covering her eyes like film. She was lying on an unfamiliar surface and scrabbled madly with one hand, the other locked inexplicably to her chest. Her fingers twisted into thick green grass, greasy with steam and engine oil, and she realised she'd been thrown out of the carriage.

Pain bolted through her entire body as she tried

to sit up. Blinking, she began to take in more of her surroundings. Her arm fell away from her chest and she moaned in agony as it flopped limply into her lap with a muted *crunch*. A throbbing ache bloomed from the broken elbow and surged into her head. She looked around.

Mountains of twisted metal and glass smashed into the hillsides, great mechanical abominations of amalgamated pistons standing like towers in the dirt. The track was smeared with coal and blood and around her the only sound was the crackling of a wildfire spreading through the trees. She had expected coughing, crying, screaming—

She staggered to her feet, clutching her broken arm, and looked around in despair. Miasmic clouds pumped across her vision and made it difficult to discern flesh from metal but she could tell that nothing was moving. Ropes of organ hung, billowing and pink, off of wooden struts that smouldered in the dawn-light. One charred body near to her gripped a burnt briefcase with knotted fingers and she saw slivers of bone between the black, blistered skin. A young girl lay with her head lolling over a great sharp slice of undercarriage, her left leg twisted awfully across her body.

Nina covered her mouth and stumbled across the wreckage, tears streaming down her face. Her broken arm dangled uselessly, fresh tendrils of pain coiling around her body as it swung beside her. Her steps were uneven and she felt a bright wet heat spreading across her stomach, but ignored it. She had to get out of the flaming valley before something else went up and it all blew. Had to get away…

"Hello?" she yelled, her voice hoarse. Looking desperately around she screamed into the heaps of ash and burnt metal. "Hello, is anyone still…"

She crumpled suddenly and fell onto her knees in the grass. Her eyes stung with tears and she wailed loudly, painfully, her whole body rocking. After a few minutes – perhaps an hour, even, maybe longer – she crawled to her feet and staggered toward the hillside, trying not to look at the mangled bodies around her.

The fingers of her good hand plunged into the dirt and she climbed awkwardly, her breathing ragged and unnatural, her chest heaving. Nina's hair was in her face and her skin felt hot and itchy, her pores weeping. Fighting her way through a cluster of white roots, she struggled to the top of the slope and hauled herself to her feet.

The trees blew behind her as she gazed up to the top of a steep hill, wind buffeting her face. The smell of smoke rose from the valley below, acrid and overwhelming. Her stomach burned. Hunger? It didn't matter. The hot, squirming pain in her abdomen was symptomatic. The disaster was below her, burning.

At the hilltop, the smudge of a dull red building was hammered on either side by angry clouds. A storm was coming.

Clutching her arm, Nina started to limp up to the farmhouse.

A thin blanket of mist rolled downhill past her ankles as Nina moved through a wall of light drizzling rain, almost relieved at the sensation of dozens of tiny, cold points peppering her exposed arms and face. Her insides were boiling, stoked like the coal in the engine, threatening to erupt at any time.

She peered into the rain, momentarily blinded by a haze of reflected sunlight. Her heart thumped her chest as she realised something was coming toward: an enormous figure had appeared in the drizzle, his shoulders thick and wide, his legs like trunks. He walked down the slope like a man who had grown up on the hillside itself, easily despite his size.

Pulse racing with relief, Nina raised her good arm and waved it frantically. Ignoring the pain in her legs she started to move faster, struggling up the incline. Plump raindrops spattered the top of her head and she felt her shirt slowly soaking. "Hey!" she yelled. "Help me! Please!"

The man paused. Nina opened her mouth to yell again but then he raised his own hand, slowly, and offered her a calm, gentle wave. Nina frowned, unsettled by the man's presence, wondering now if she should turn back and just crawl back into the wreckage. What was he doing out here? He must have heard the crash, he realised, and was wandering down to take a look. Well, he could bloody well wander a little faster…

"I need help," she croaked, staggering on weak legs. "I think… I don't think anybody else got out. Please, you have to help me…"

Nina stopped when she was half a dozen feet

from the man, her eyes locked on his. There was something in his face that made her uneasy, an expression of sorrow that looked as if it were built on years and years of heartache.

"Help," she started again, pointing vaguely down at the valley. "The train crashed – there was another… why are you looking at me like that?"

The man blinked. Slowly, he reached into his shirt and withdrew a yellowed newspaper.

"What are you doing? There might be people down there, I need you to…" Her eyes flickered from his face to the paper and back again. "What is that? Why are you just standing there? Please, help me—"

The man ran a hand through his wet hair, sweeping it out of his eyes.

He smiled sadly at her, then took another step forward and offered her the paper.

"Morning, Nina," he said softly.

"What?" Nina whispered, confused. "How do you… what is this?"

"It's okay," he said.

"Listen, I just—"

"—need my help, you're not sure what happened but you think everyone's dead," the man supplied, his voice low and soft, somehow comforting and mournful all at once.

"That's not… I was—"

"—going to say exactly that," he finished.

"How are you doing that?"

"I'm sorry," he said, taking another step closer and thrusting the newspaper toward her. "I've done this so many times, and I'm… oh, god, forgive me, I'm tired. This is the easiest way to do it."

Nina looked down at the paper. After a moment, she snatched it from him.

Her heart turned to ice.

HORROR CRASH ON NORFOLK RAILWAY; NO SURVIVORS

"Wait, I—"

"Look at the date," the man said sombrely.

Nina looked. The newspaper felt old, the paper almost flaking, the ink smudged in places, the corners creased and folded. But the date…

"22nd July, 1942," she whispered. "That's…"

"Tomorrow," he said. "Am I right?"

She looked at him. "What's happening?"

"That paper is over eighty years old," the man said quietly. "I'm sorry, Nina, I'm so sorry, but… you didn't make it."

Nina shook her head. "What the hell does that mean? It *just* happened, I'm… I'm alive. I'm right here in front of you. The train is down there—"

"Look, then," the man nodded. "Look at it."

Nina hesitated. Something drizzled down her abdomen. "No," she said eventually, her voice a whisper.

"Please, Nina, don't make this any harder than it has to be," the man said. "Look down at the tracks."

Slowly, Nina turned her head. Before she could look into the valley she whipped it back again, squeezing her eyes shut. "No. Something's wrong, none of this makes any sense…"

"Nina, look."

After a few moments, she opened her eyes and looked down.

At the base of the hill, the railway tracks curled around in a dreadful scar of dry earth and steel. The snaking, burning bodies of two colossal trains lay strangling each other, plumes of smoke and fire drifting lazily up around them. She could smell burning bodies from here, the dreadful stench of charred meat fusing with steam and petrichor all around her.

Both trains flickered in and out of existence as she watched, their awful snake-like forms blurring into shadow before reforming again. They weren't real, she saw. The hillside, the valley… all of this was solid and colourful, but the wreckage…

The wreckage had long since been cleared away, the lines repaired.

As she watched, figures began to appear, standing up in the wreckage and turning toward her. One by one they started to stagger up the slope, just as she had done. Flickering all the while, blurring and clarifying, liquefying and twisting back into shape.

"I'm sorry," Hamish whispered.

Still gripping the paper, she shook her head and stared. "But I'm…"

"No," he said. "Look down, Nina. Your stomach."

Nina blinked. She didn't need to look down to know what she'd see – a part of her had known, she realised, all along – but nonetheless she tipped her chin to her chest and gazed down.

A long spear of shrapnel had been buried in her belly, and blood drooled out of the wound and down her legs. The pain, she realised now, was unbearable.

"Every day the *Circadia* comes along," Hamish said softly, "and every day the *Titan* crashes into it. It took them weeks to investigate, but eventually they found out what had happened. A faulty signal, that was all. Two trains on the same track, racing along in opposite directions… just an accident. And everybody died."

The hillside was crawling with figures now, every shape bleeding and smoking and burned. All confused and terrified, every passenger bewildered to find themselves walking upright despite their massive injuries.

"I'm so, so sorry."

"Everything was going to be better," Nina said hoarsely, looking at Hamish. "Today… today was the day everything changed."

Hamish smiled sadly at her. He was crying, she saw suddenly, his eyes brimming with water.

"You… you do this every day? Come down

here and tell us all what really happened?"

"I never had much experience with ghosts till my father died," Hamish shook his head. "And now… yeah. Every day. They're confused, you see. All of them. Just like you. And if I'm not here to comfort them… to try and help them pass on…"

"Does it work?" Nina said. "Do we ever… have any of us ever…"

"Not yet," Hamish said. "But I'm working on it."

"I don't want to do this again," Nina whispered, staring down into the wreckage as it smouldered, only semi-visible in the haze and the fog.

"I know," Hamish said. He reached out and gripped her hand, though the sensation was unnatural and only semi-tangible. "That's just what you said yesterday."

CROSSING

Thick ribbons of soot knotted the steam puffing from the locomotive's funnel; with an unhealthy rattle the engine choked on its own black cloud, the coaches behind it shuddering on the rails as the train ground to a stop. Pistons screamed as the wheels slowed from one-thirty miles per hour to zero in less than eight seconds; there was a cacophony of yelps and muffled thumps as the passengers were tossed about in their compartments. More than one of the glass doors separating each booth slid open on their runners.

Another few seconds and the locomotive was entirely dead. The last wheezing protests of the engine fell silent and the chuntering rattle of the train's grease-spattered underbelly followed. The old steam engine had been pulling its load up a steep incline, the rails clinging to the mountainside fitted with derailment protection devices so that the train's wheels couldn't slip off. Now it lay mid-crawl, the automatic brakes engaged, steam clotting angrily in the funnel; still, silent, stopped.

The mountain wall loomed up above the train, blood-red and streaked with white, clumps of moss bright green in the sparkling sunlight. A little way ahead of the engine, a foamy spit of water dribbled down the sheer cliff and into a deep pool dozens of feet beneath the sandstone bridge that carried the rails; here the water turned a glittering blue and streamed toward a ragged outcrop, where it spilled down into the valley below. The locomotive had stopped right at the beginning of the bridge, the engine overhanging it by a few sleepers, as though it had begun to chew its way across and filled its belly a little quicker than expected.

There was commotion in first class.

The conductor passed from booth to booth, knocking on each glass partition before sliding it open to check that the passengers inside were unharmed and – more importantly – not dissatisfied with their trip. He made it very clear to every red-faced businessman that there was nothing wrong with the train, and that he was certain there must be something on the line that would be cleared momentarily. One woman had spilled red wine across her furs and he offered promptly to take it away and have it cleaned in the service carriage, but she haughtily declined. He quickly shut the glass door and moved to the next booth.

Of course, there was nothing on the line. Nothing wrong with the train, either, not as far as the bewildered driver and fireman in the engine room could see, though there must be *something*; why else should the locomotive stop at the first sign of running water?

The conductor brushed his lapel and knocked patiently on the glass partition of a booth on the left of the coach, about halfway along. "Excuse me, sir?"

The gentleman inside might have been asleep, for he was huddled in one corner of the compartment with a thick, black cloak pulled up over his face. But he was laid in such a position that the conductor wondered if he might have been knocked unconscious by the impact of the locomotive's sudden standstill, and so he persisted.

"Sir?"

After a moment more he slid open the door and stepped into the compartment, cringing at the sudden chill he felt the moment he crossed the threshold. It was like passing into an icebox. Glancing up, he saw that the large, round-cornered window above the sleeping gentleman was open, and he briskly reached across the compartment to pull it closed. In doing so he caught sight of the vista beyond the window and was hit with a sudden bolt of vertigo: behind them, the cliff lurched up into a cloudless, blue sky; looking out of this window, however, he saw nothing but the endless drop to the bottom of the valley.

"Sir," he said again, stepping back from the window and laying a hand gently on the man's shoulder. "I don't mean to disturb you, but…"

He trailed off, a queer uneasiness settling in his stomach and clawing impatiently at the lining. His skin prickled, every hair raising at once. There was something wrong here, he thought, looking over the sleeping figure on the smartly-upholstered bench. The man must have been tall, for even slumped in his cloak like this he was an imposing figure; little of him was visible beneath the cloak but the conductor could see pale, bony fingers curled around a fold of the material and noted that they were almost entirely white in colour, only tinged with the faintest hints of blue at the joints.

"Sir," the conductor said, a little louder. Steeling himself, he reached down to pull back the unconscious fellow's cloak.

He gasped as the man's face was unveiled. Slick, black hair peeled back from a sallow brow, his eyes sunk into deep pits. They were open wide and didn't blink or flicker when they were uncovered; the man's chest was moveless. His skin was the same faintly-bruised, almost translucent white as his thin fingers.

He was dead.

The conductor balked, raising a hand to his mouth. He turned away to vomit, but not before registering a strange mar on the man's exposed throat: two faint, purple spots, like the puncture wounds left by a venomous snake's bite—

The glass partition rattled open and he looked up, quite certain that his own face must have gone an awful shade of white.

The woman with the wine-stained furs stepped into the compartment, smiling warmly as she slid the door closed behind her. The conductor caught a brief flash of white as the sharp, white points in her gums glinted in the sunlight.

"I don't think this train is going anywhere while I'm on board," the woman said quietly, and the conductor realised, all too late, that the spatters of crimson across her chest were far too dark to be wine. Beneath the train he heard the ever-so-faint roar of rushing water. Cries of brusque dismay from farther down the carriage.

The woman grinned, flashing those sharp, sharp teeth again.

"So I thought I'd have a little snack before I alight," she whispered, and she bore down on him like thunder.

SHADOWS OVER CULLING STREET STATION

The 9:46 to Cambridge pulled up at Culling Hill's only platform three minutes late, just as the winter sun was cresting the shingled roof of the station building. Light from the bristling white orb splashed the blank, glassy face of the engine and beamed off rivets along the carriages' paintwork. The windows were dark.

The train slowed and stopped with a pneumatic hiss and a final *kunk-kunk* of settling wheels; the platform was otherwise silent. Passengers seldom boarded at Culling Hill, save for those who'd woken early for the commuter-heavy train at 6:30, or the odd middle-aged parent heading into town for their weekly shop. The trains were usually unreliable and often more expensive than driving – and, of course, most of the people who wanted to leave Culling Hill in a more substantial sense had either already left, or realised they never would.

Finally moveless, the Class 745 lay quietly on the rails, an enormous petrified serpent with red-and-yellow piping. The sleepers beneath it were damp and mottled with clumps of green weeds and thistles; the gravel was marred with sludgy smears of grit and littered with rat droppings. The platform itself was a cracked heap of concrete decorated with faded yellow lines and a pair of sagging benches, each one dipping toward the middle of the station as though pulled into the gravitational field of a great sinkhole right beneath the door of the station building.

The door swung open suddenly and a figure stumbled out, hastily working his belt buckle. Dressed in the crisp, dark uniform of a British Rail conductor, his hair was combed neatly, the stubble on his face deliberately trimmed to an eight of an inch. His eyes were wide with panic.

"Agh, god, sorry," Jones called loudly, "I heard you were running a few minutes late and thought I'd take a leak – but I'm here, you're…"

Looking up, he saw that the train was still, the doors open, and that he was alone.

"...relieved," he finished.

Looking up and down the platform, he was almost stunned by the stillness of it all. Nobody had alighted, though a full minute must have passed since he'd heard the train pull up from within the bathroom cubicle in his office. There was no sign of Gareth Dixon, the conductor from whom he was scheduled to take over. Even the birds that usually nested in the clumpy hedge spilling across the rails at the end of the platform had fallen silent.

"Gary?" he said, calling shyly into the open carriage door nearest to him. "I'm here, if you want to step off. Shift's over, buddy."

Nothing from inside. He stepped forward, zipping up his fly as discretely as possible in case anybody was watching him from within the carriage. The ticket machine at his waist swung a little as he leaned in, glancing furtively into the train.

"Gary?"

The coach was silent, as though completely empty. From down on the platform he could only see the backs of the nearest seats, but he was certain that there must be *somebody* on board; the

9:46 was never busy, but it was usually at least a third of the way to capacity. There was no chatter, no tinny, muffled whine of headphone music. No Gareth Dixon.

"Well, never mind then," Jones huffed quietly, stepping on board. Dixon was probably in the loo, or having another argument with a passenger. Well, these people had places to be; the train was already delayed, and it was up to him to get them going again. "Right then—"

The train jolted as, with another hiss of hydraulic fluid, the doors clamped shut behind him. Jones bolted out of his skin and wheeled around, looking down the aisle toward the front of the train as if he'd be able to see right into the engine.

Without any signal from him, the train jerked to a start and began to roll loudly along the rails. For a moment Jones stood by the door, dumbfounded, then he shook his head and braced himself above the rattling wheels. Straightening his jacket, he laid a hand on the ticket machine and stepped forward. "Tickets at the ready, please," he called loudly. "Tickets, everybody…"

He trailed off as the train rocked gently beneath

him and he looked into the coach. Before him, a carpeted blue aisle stretched to the other end of the narrow compartment, a worn snakeskin sloughed off and abandoned. Either side of it, hard-backed seats with crazy bowling-alley carpet upholstery were arranged in pairs, either side of smooth plastic tables. About half of them were full; that wasn't particularly unexpected.

But everybody – every single passenger – was asleep, and that was unprecedented.

At first, he didn't notice what each passenger was holding in their lap; that would come momentarily. For now he was equal parts bemused and uneasy, and when he reached out for the rail beside him to steady himself it was only partly because of the train's movements. Looking around at all these people asleep in their seats – heads bowed, eyes closed, but none of them snoring, not one – he couldn't help but sense that something was... *off*.

Letting go of the rail, he backed up a step and turned around, heading for the partition behind him. Raising a hand to his brow, Jones leaned forward and squinted through the tiny window, his body shuddering with the train as he looked into the next carriage.

Everybody in there was asleep, too.

Drawing in a deep breath, Jones turned again and propelled himself determinedly into the coach, clearing his throat loudly. He lifted the ticket machine in one hand and moved the fingers of the other to its flaking, laminated keypad. "All right, everybody," he said loudly, "tickets, please!"

Green shapes raked past the windows as the train flashed through fields and burrowed down a shallow incline toward the next village. Steep, crumbling verges either side of the rails were clawed through with smudged strokes of brown and grey, gnarled roots dug into the ground that, in time, would unsettle the sleepers and churn the whole railway out of the earth.

"Tickets!" Jones called again, louder still, then under his breath he cursed Dixon for leaving him with this less-than-rowdy bunch of weirdos. He lamented the late-night services for the drunkenness and callous remarks of the football crowd; this particular service he was beginning to dislike even more potently for quite the opposite reason.

Taking a slow, cautious step forward, Jones

leaned toward the nearest passenger and laid a hand gently on her shoulder.

The moment the pads of his fingers touched her cardigan, his whole body stiffened as though electrocuted. A sharp, bright bolt of pain shot into his skull and his eyes rolled up in their sockets; head tipped back, he saw stars.

He saw an entire universe.

At once he was elsewhere, somewhere he had never been but that he felt, intimately, he might have come from. The deep wet pitch of space swum around him and he watched galaxies unfurl, systems of bright white points expanding and collapsing in on themselves. It was vast, endless, like those telescope pictures but in a million colours he shouldn't be able to see; in less than half a second he had travelled lightyears, and he knew his lungs should have had all the air sucked out of them, knew that his skin should have frozen and solidified and cracked—

But he was still.

Something moved. A titanic shape, gently unfolding from the fabric of space, extending long, curled arms into distances that Jones couldn't fathom. It was everywhere and nowhere; he couldn't see it so much as see the void where it should have been: being able to see it, he knew, would have been so much worse than simply knowing it was there.

A colossal eye opened in the midst of the thing, an orb of absolute white shot through with veins of every colour imaginable and surrounded by starlit teeth.

The thing began to speak, and its voice, though inaudible, rippled through Jones' entire body like water poured into his throat; it said, "*Get them—*"

Then Jones's body wobbled back as the train swooped around a sheer bend in the rails and he let go of the woman's shoulder, his palm disconnecting with the material of her cardigan and just as instantly severing his connection with the swirling, infinite vortex of which, just for a moment, he'd been a part.

He blinked.

Taking a stumbling step back and scrambling for the rail, he realised his entire body was shaking. Though he couldn't see his reflection in any of the nearby windows he knew that his hair was on end as though he'd rubbed two balloons together and then jammed a lit firework into his urethra; his blood felt instantaneously too warm and too cold.

"What the…"

Jones focused on bringing himself back into the present, assuring himself that he'd take a mental inventory of every drink he'd consumed over the last twenty-four hours just as soon as his legs stopped buckling beneath him. The experience had lasted less than a second, he was convinced of it, but he felt as though he'd been staring into that unfurling, tentacled plane of existence for centuries.

"*Next stop: Rinford and Hack,*" squawked the intercom behind his ear and Jones almost shrieked, staggering away from the rail and into the aisle. They could only have been a couple minutes from the next village, and he hadn't stamped a single ticket; well, how could he, if everyone was asleep?

His stomach twisted suddenly into a very tight, very painful knot as he realised that perhaps they weren't asleep after all. Wheeling around, he stumbled farther into the carriage and steadied himself on the headrest of an aisle seat, gripping it with white knuckles. He looked down into the booth and saw a family sitting around the table: a young, Black boy and girl on one side, and two women in what Jones presumed were their mid-thirties across from them. They all sat with their hands in their laps, almost entirely obscured, and all four heads were lowered so that he had to lean forward to see that their eyes were, indeed, closed.

For a moment he stood staring at the chest of the nearest woman, terrified that she might wake up any moment and think him perverted – but aware, to his even greater terror, that she didn't seem likely to – and noted that there was movement. Breath. She was alive. Shifting his gaze to the chest of the young boy, he saw the same.

Alive, all of them. But unconscious.

"Hello," he said quietly, "excuse me, I just need to—"

Something twitched suddenly in the boy's lap, enfolded in his hands. Jones' eyes fell onto the thing and he balked.

"Oh, god, what in the name of…"

The boy's stubby fingers were curled tightly around something that looked a little like a spider, its long, thin legs folded over his hands; but the spider's skin was rubbery and wet and it had too many legs, two dozen perhaps before Jones lost count. It twitched and convulsed, almost pulsing like a beating heart, and as Jones looked from the boy's lap to his sister's he saw that she was holding one too.

And something else, something that he couldn't believe he hadn't seen before; was he out of his mind? Or was something else *in* it, something with the power to stop him from seeing things that didn't want to be seen?

The children's lips were parted, and from each of their mouths spooled a long, black tendril. Saliva dribbled down the boy's tendril as it fell into his lap and swung up into his hand; the girl's did the same, connecting her mouth to the thing in her tight, determined grip.

Swinging his head toward their parents, Jones saw that the two women also held little dark spidery things, and the thin black umbilical cords connecting those things to something inside their throats were also present.

They had vomited them up, he realised.

"Oh, god," he said, standing straight and turning his head. More of the tentacled things in the hands of the man and woman sitting in the next booth;

more, still, in the hands of an elderly woman in the next row. She had been reading a newspaper when she'd thrown up the creature and it lay beneath her clasped, gnarled fingers in her lap, spattered with drops of dark, oily fluid.

Jones turned back to the family beside him and swallowed nervously.

Gingerly, he reached down with a trembling hand and moved to pry open the nearest woman's fingers, hoping for a better look at the thing she was holding—

Instantly he was thrown into that elsewhere-place again, his head smacked back, his eyes poked back into his skull by invisible fingers. In the tiny fraction of a second that he was there he saw it move, that endless, tentacled creature, saw it coil its arms around galaxies and crush them into oblivion, saw the rings of teeth around its shining white eye retract into void-like gums and pierce them again. Heard its voice, like thunder:

"*—somewhere they—*"

Then he ripped his hand away and lurched back into the carriage, his head pounding.

"Fuck my mouth," he whispered, grabbing the seat again to support his suddenly-leaden body. He doubled over to throw up and his eyes widened as he saw the thing in the aisle, the thing that had fallen out of the woman's hands when he'd sprung the fingers open.

It wriggled slowly, dozens of tiny, snake-like arms writhing and poking at the air. Its flesh was like oil, a tiny mouth in the middle of its body opening and shutting as it pulsed wetly. The size of a dormouse or a small bird, it looked like…

God, it looked like a *baby*…

Still connected to the woman's throat by the long, black cord that spilled out from between her lips, the creature twisted its body in something that looked like pain, and as Jones watched, its tentacles folded in and it *sucked*. The thin, wet cable bulged as something passed through it, and the creature's body bloomed with colour as it absorbed that something, strengthened by it.

It was feeding off of *her*, Jones realised. It had come out of her and now it was sucking the life out of her. Out of all of them. How many people were on this train? And how many of these creatures – these *things* – would he find if he looked?

get them somewhere they

"No," Jones murmured, backing away. He

staggered to the back of the carriage and slammed his back against the wall, shaking his head. "No, no, no, no, no—"

There was a sick *schlopp* sound and something dropped into the air inches from his face, reminding him briefly of one of those aircraft safety videos where the oxygen mask plummets from the ceiling on a thick, white cable; except the thing that had dropped was another of the tiny, multiple-armed creatures and the cable was a long, thin black cord, gluey with saliva—

The creature opened its mouth and hissed, all its tentacles lashing back at once as though it meant to strike him with them. Mania pulsing through his blood, Jones launched his fist forward before he could stop himself and punched the thing square in its tiny, wet mouth. It screeched as it swung back on its cord and Jones was thrust into the elsewhere of space, just long enough for him to hear the great vast creature above say *NEED* and then he was back, his body cold with fear, his head tipped back – and finally, he found Gareth Dixon.

The conductor's skin had been drained of colour and his arms were bent back, his fingers suckered to the ceiling. His eyes were gone and around the edges of the sockets tiny black tentacles wriggled and slapped the skin of his cheeks. The shrieking creature that Jones had punched swung lazily from Dixon's open mouth.

Thick, dark shapes moved beneath the man's skin, worms in his bloodstream. Immediately Jones knew that the other conductor had been presented with the same task

get them somewhere they need

as him, and he knew that Dixon had refused – or failed – and he realised that the very same thing would happen to him if he did so.

Jones hesitated. Beneath him the train shuddered along the rails, and all around the world blurred by.

Slowly, he nodded. Looking up into Dixon's mouth, he whispered, "What do I do?"

When no answer came, he reached up with a shaking hand and laid it against the conductor's cheek.

"—*to be,*" finished the endless creature, and he understood. He saw, in the deepest pit of black beneath the beast's abominable reach, a single star pop into existence, a tiny point of white in the deep. And he watched as more bloomed into life around it, watched them spread, fill the emptiness with light, watched them seep through the universe.

Pulling himself back to reality – the reality that he knew – Jones ducked under the creature swinging pendulum-like from Dixon's throat and stepped forward.

Get them somewhere they need to be.

No, that wasn't right. That wasn't what the creature had meant, he thought; it didn't matter where they went next. It didn't matter how many stops they took, or to where the train was headed as its final destination. It only mattered that there were people at the end of the line.

They would spread, and consume, but they needed people.

Get them somewhere, the creatures' unholy father had told him.

And, separately:

They need to be.

JANE

RODE

THE

RAILWAY

Red clots of sand billowed out behind the leviathan as it thundered along the rails, a streamlined beast of polished rivets and smouldering heat. Explosions of sound smacked the pistons as they wheezed back and forth, fragments of stone punching into the wooden sleepers as the great train ground a devastating path through the landscape, enormous black clouds of soot unfolding from its funnel and darkening a boiling yellow sky.

The dining cart was half-full and awash with a gentle bloom of chatter, polite passengers speaking quietly to their new acquaintances across the aisle as families ate and laughed and played cards in a cloying fog of cigar smoke. The windows were streaked with colour, distant mountains and rocky outcrops blurring into smudges of clay-coloured nothingness as smatterings of sand and dirt drily splashed the greasy glass. The carriage shook and shuddered, a great rattling beneath the passengers' seats booming in time with erratic and bone-shaking vibrations.

At the rear end of the coach, tucked so far into the corner of her booth that she faded almost entirely into the wallpapered backdrop behind her, a slight, tired-eyed woman in a black dress and veil sat quietly.

As they knifed through the barren plains of the west the passengers indulged heartily in wine and beef as though they knew, somehow, that something was about to happen. Gas lamps burned hungrily on their brackets, filaments sizzling orange inside orbs of scorched glass; plush crimson curtains were pinned back from the windows to let in the light, and the carpet was dappled with soft amber shadows. The edges of tables and seats glinted sharply.

A gunslinger sat alone at a table near the front of the carriage, swaying gently in his seat as the train lumbered violently across the desert. His bearded face was bathed in the shadow of a wide-brimmed hat, square jaw resting on a fist wrapped in tatty red cloth. His eyes were fixed on the window and he gazed absent-mindedly through it, watching a hungry pack of vultures swarm a distant carcass, the savaged husk of some once-great beast lying prone in the sand and twitching as they ripped at its meaty throat. A revolver swung matter-of-factly from his belt, only half-obscured by the folds of a great leather coat. Every now and then his gaze would leave the window and scour the tables throughout the carriage. Each time he looked around his eyes would land upon the shrewish woman at the opposite end of the coach, and he would pause, try to discern her features through the lacy haze of her veil, give up, and return his attention to the glass. Deadeyed Danny Harrigan was a naturally suspicious man who had already assessed all the other passengers and found them unthreatening; she was an enigma, but there was no sense staring an enigma down until it moved.

Eventually it would, and until that time, he would keep his eyes on the reflections in the glass.

Across from him, there was a sudden shattering of glass.

"You big lard-faced buffoon!" hissed a bald, dark-skinned woman as she recoiled from the man sitting across from her, lifting her foot out of a glassy mess of wine already seeping into the carpet. Apologetically her partner, a well-built man in pinstripes and a flocked black bowler, reached down to clear up the mess. She swiped at his hand. "You lay off, Jack! Keep your god-damn hands to yourself, willya?"

Quietly, the gunslinger chuckled. The well-built man glanced up, apparently not hard of hearing, already reddening in the cheeks. "Something funny there, stranger?" he said, eyes narrowing to beady pinkish points.

The gunslinger half-raised his hand in apology and returned his attention to the window, immediately falling silent. Halfway down the carriage a family of four – two girls and their parents, all bundled around a near-finished game of Faro – fell quiet too, stunned into a temporary unease by the sudden commotion.

"Jack, will you go and fetch the darned conductor?" the bald Black woman exclaimed, wiggling her foot out of the soiled shoe and tutting as she nearly pressed her heel into a slim, curved shard of glass.

"Now, hang on a minute," well-built Jack said, rising to his feet and stepping into the aisle, his eyes still on the gunslinger. One finger raised, he gripped the back of the nearest seat to steady himself as the carriage shuddered. "What's so funny, big shot?"

The gunslinger sighed and turned back to the man. "I must apologise," he said slowly, his gruff voice a quiet rumble. "I'd not meant to laugh at your expense, sir. Please forgive me."

Well-built Jack folded his arms. "I might forgive you if you'd tell me what in tarnation you was laughing at, *sir*."

The gunslinger gritted his teeth. Quite deliberately, he brushed his knuckles against the lapel of his coat and nudged it aside, putting his piece on full display. "I'd encourage you to sit back down, mister."

Jack swallowed. Beside him his partner reached out, grabbing his sleeve. "Sit, idiot," she hissed.

"Fine," Jack said haughtily.

"Good boy," said the gunslinger, turning his head. As he did he noticed that the lithe woman at the back of the carriage had moved; she was checking her watch, a fine brass piece latched to a skinny, black-clad wrist. In fact, he noted, not an inch of her wasn't covered in black, for she also wore slim, leather gloves. Glancing up out of the window, he saw that the bloated sun was still high in the sky and sweating hard: the train was running right to schedule. What was she so worried about that she had to check the time? His suspicions hardened and he shifted uncomfortably in his seat.

Halfway down the carriage, the family had returned to their game.

"I wonder if we oughtn't move carriages," Arnold Cullen whispered quietly to his wife, keeping his eyes on the gunslinger as, the other side of the table, his daughters giggled over their cards. "If something breaks out between those two hardasses, I'd rathern't be—"

"Oh, do hush," Ria Cullen whispered back. "Let's just focus on our business, shall we? And then nobody'll bother us."

"All right," Arnold said, then, grinning to the two girls, he said, "Who'd like to call it a day on this hand and play dice instead? Chuck-a-luck, Alice? What about you, Ruby? Chuck-a-luck? High-low?"

Nine-year-old Ruby beamed, eyes glinting mischievously as sunlight streamed off her curls. "Just because you're *losing*, Daddy!"

"Yeah, I'm not changing game!" said the younger of the girls, Alice, slapping her cards down on the table. "Just because you're *losing*!"

"Shhh," Ria whispered gleefully to her daughters, shoulders tucked in as she lunged forward with a cheeky spark in her eyes. "You know, I think we ought to beat your daddy quickly, don't we? Put him out of his—"

There was a sudden scream of metal on metal and the carriage shuddered violently. At once the streaking shades of clay-red and burnt ochre flitting past the windows began to slow. The train was slowing down.

"Christ, what on Earth?" Jack said gruffly, drawing the gunslinger's attention again. "Poppy, where the hell are we? We're not stopping here, are we?"

"How in damnation should I know?" his partner scolded.

"Look!" piped up a shrill voice near the back of the carriage. The gunslinger cocked an eyebrow, looking up to see that a small, oily businessman with a thin moustache and a lit cigar in his hand had stood up from his seat and was pointing out of the window. "God in Heaven, look out there!"

The carriage rocked again as the train slowed almost to a stop. Ria Cullen clamped a hand over her mouth, stifling a scream as her eyes moved to the window. Elsewhere in the carriage another man cried out, two women behind him scrambling to their feet.

The train stuttered, the rattling, booming sound beneath them finally stopping.

There was stillness. Silence.

Disturbed, the gunslinger slowly turned his head to look in the direction the little businessman had pointed.

The plains stretched out before him, vast and yellow and pocked with marks of green and grey where dead plants curled into themselves, clawed branches scratching uselessly at their own insides. Blood-soaked mountains poked relentlessly at pure-white clouds, the sky bristling with a wall of shimmering heat.

A long, black carriage had pulled up alongside the train, two steers braying aggressively against their reins as a string of men in dark clothes unloaded from the back, leaping down into the sand. Deadeyed Danny Harrigan watched through narrowed eyes as two masked thugs smashed the already-bloodied train driver into the dirt, while another trained a long, black rifle on the engine's fireman. More began to climb onto the first-class carriage, whooping and swinging revolvers with wild abandon.

"Fucking bandits," Harrigan murmured, fingering his own piece.

An explosion of sound from the front of the train drew his attention to the carriage door. A gunshot, louder than thunder. Behind him, one of the men screamed. Ria and Arnold Cullen bundled their kids together, nudging them under the table as they gripped each other tightly. Well-built Jack had retreated as far into his booth as he could while Poppy reached a hand into her corset and withdrew a small, ivory-handled six-shooter, her jaw hard and set.

At the back of the coach, the woman in the black veil sat completely still, unfazed by the attack.

There was silence for a moment, and then a colossal explosion from the back of the train. The carriage buckled and another gunshot rang out from outside: the driver was face-down in the dirt, blood pooling from a wound in his chest. The gunslinger waited. *One.*

Two.

Three...

The carriage door swung open.

Three shapes stomped into the coach, accompanied by the stench of gunsmoke and blood. There was screaming, immediately silenced as one of the figures steamed forward and raised her revolver. "We will have some god-damn *quiet*!" yelled a second, reaching up a hand to remove the tattered bandana covering her face.

The third moved halfway down the carriage, swinging a sawn-off shotgun left and right before turning round and raising a bloody fist. The gunslinger saw a serrated hunting knife clamped to her belt as the breeze through the open carriage door lifted the corner of her coat.

Slowly, he stood.

"Listen here," he said confidently, slowly reaching for his piece. The nearest of the bandits turned her eyes on him, thick sharp tufts of red hair falling in her face as she reached up to tip back her hat. The gunslinger continued: "You want money, right? Well, listen to me, there'll be no—"

"Shut up!" hissed the bandit with the shotgun, swinging it suddenly and pumping the trigger. The carriage exploded with sound and a spray of shot blasted the gunslinger in the face, punching it out through the back of his skull and splashing the window with red mist. He crumpled, swaying on his knees for a moment before slumping onto his stomach.

He convulsed once, then was still.

Across the carriage, Jack yelled out and drew his legs awkwardly onto his seat, as if avoiding the pooling blood would save him from anything worse.

"We are not here for money!" the red-haired bandit called calmly, raising both hands and stepping forward. Elsewhere on the train, another gunshot rang out. Muffled, agonised screams rang out on the wind as it billowed softly into the carriage. "Get your purses back in your pockets, get your asses back in your seats, and listen up!"

The bandit with the revolver started to move between the tables, gesturing for silence with one finger while she pointed her piece deliberately from one face to the next, her thumb permanently poised on the hammer.

"We are here," the bandit continued, turning back to close the door softly, "on behalf of Sheriff Sam Dutton. Some of you may have heard of our employer; some of you may have *met*—"

"That nutcase?" the businessman near the back of the carriage piped up shrilly. "What does he want with us?"

"Not 'us'," the bandit smiled thinly. "Just one of you."

"Sit your fucking ass down," said the woman with the sawn-off shotgun, swinging it in the businessman's direction.

"Now, some of you may know that Sheriff Dutton is somewhat of a collector in his off-time," the bandit said, walking slowly down the aisle. "A collector of the *para-normal*. Items of particular significance to him are those which have been possessed. Haunted. Cast down to this realm from another, or *up* from Hell. He has paid us a handsome sum—"

"—very handsome—"

"—for the capture of a particularly elusive item."

Another gunshot from the farthest end of the

train. Slowly, the pistons beneath the carriage began to grind together, pumping forward as the fire in the engine was stoked. A thick, shuddering rattle began to vibrate through the carriage as the train slowly moved forward, gaining speed as it started to move past the driver and fireman, both dead in the dirt outside. The bandits had taken over the engine. Whatever they wanted from the train, it was valuable enough that they'd paid no mind to leaving their own cart and horses behind.

"Now," said the red-haired bandit slowly, her eyes settling on the lithe figure at the very back of the carriage. Through the haze of her black veil, the woman stared back. The bandit winked. "Is that you, Jane?"

The woman in the veil said nothing. Didn't even shift in her seat. She sat, a slight and unassuming figure totally unbothered by the stink of blood that rose like the tang of pennies on the air. The third bandit jabbed the barrel of her shotgun in the woman's direction, but still nothing.

"Will you come quietly?" said the red-haired bandit.

There was a long silence, and then the woman in the veil blinked. Slowly, she reached up to lift it away from her face.

Dragging it above her lips, which were pale and bloodless, she whispered, "I always do."

The bandit's face twisted into one of blank surprise as a bullet soared through the top of her skull, chipping a red-raw chunk of flesh out of her forehead. Her breath hitched in her throat and she toppled forward, the sound of the blast echoing through the carriage. The train thundered forward, building up speed and ploughing into the desert as the red-haired woman's limp body tumbled into the nearest chair with a loud *kunk* and slid to the floor. Halfway down the carriage the bandit with the revolver wheeled around, her eyes wide with shock. Looking up past the body of her comraded she yelled angrily, jabbing down the hammer and preparing to fire—

Poppy stepped out into the aisle, aiming her piece with both hands and gently squeezing the trigger. The six-shooter cracked open loudly, punching a bullet down the middle of the carriage and into the bandit's chest. The bald Black woman looked coldly down the barrel as she thumbed the hammer again and the chamber stuttered round. As the second bandit was falling, blood spilling from the hole in her chest, Poppy trained the gun on the third.

"I'll fucking kill you for that!" yelled the bandit with the shotgun, lifting it high.

"Nope," Poppy said, squeezing the trigger a third time.

There was a dreadful, too-loud *click* and her heart skipped a beat. The six-shooter had jammed in her hand. Stammering, she fumbled with the gun and tried again, jamming back the trigger as her hand began to shake.

Click.

"Problem with your piece?" the bandit said spitefully. "Here, take a look at mine—"

Suddenly Arnold Cullen lurched out of his seat, scooping up the shotgun barrel with one arm and punching it upward. There was a titanic bang and the bandit's head exploded, spattering the ceiling along with most of Cullen's hand. He screamed, immediately clutching at the mess of his palm with his good hand and turning back to his wife. "Jesus!" he yelled.

Well-built Jack finally blinked. His face had been sprayed with blood; otherwise, it was completely white.

Tearing his eyes off of Poppy's body, he stumbled blindly into the aisle and bent down to pick up her gun. Nearly slipping on the blood pooling at his feet, he removed the chamber, spun it and slammed it back in.

Somebody was sobbing. The train thundered forward, the driver oblivious to everything that had happened in the dining cart. Beneath one of the tables, two young girls quivered fearfully.

Calmly, Jack walked down the aisle and raised the gun.

"Why did they want you?" he said weakly, training the barrel on the woman with the black veil. It had fallen back over her face, but he could tell she was smiling. His hand trembled as he thumbed down the hammer. "Why did Sheriff Sam Dutton want you? What kind of super-natural *hell-fiend*—"

The woman stood.

Jack backed up a step, suddenly more afraid than he had been of the bandits. A distant explosion barely registered; he watched as she moved gently around the edge of her table, stepped into the aisle, and laid a hand on his arm. Even through the black leather of her glove, she was cool to the touch.

"Watch," she whispered.

Slowly she moved past him, bending down beside the limp, bloodied body of the shotgun-wielding bandit. Delicately, she reached up and removed her veil. Jack couldn't see her face, not from this angle, but he saw what happened next.

He retched as he watched her draw in a deep breath, laying her hand on the dead woman's chest.

After a moment, the corpse twisted. There was a crack of bone and a soft, low whisper, then a sound like chunks of wood breaking, snapping, crunching. The acrid smell of death rose into the air as a thin, weeping cloud of black slipped out of the body's nostrils and mouth.

The woman in the veil drank it in, her lips parting slightly. Black fog rose into her lungs and she swallowed.

The body went still again.

Jack watched, dumbfounded, as she moved from body to body, finally stopping at the end of the carriage where Poppy lay still. Ria Cullen had turned her face away but she couldn't help but watch. Her husband had evidently forgotten the pain in his hand, and he couldn't look anywhere else but in the direction of the black-clothed woman.

She was Death, and her spell was unbearable.

Kneeling over Poppy's corpse, she looked up into Jack's eyes and smiled thinly. Her face, now fully revealed, was as pale as alabaster and deeply scarred, rivets of tissue running between her eyes and jaggedly crisscrossing each other. Her pupils were tiny: miniature black points in a sea of pale green.

Gently she breathed in, and Poppy was undone. Clots of sooty fog ripped out of her, slipping through her teeth, out of her nose and wide-open eyes and pouring quickly into Jane's throat.

The Angel of Death drunk in the woman's spirit, and when it was done, it stood.

"Dutton wanted me for his collection," she whispered. "I don't belong to him."

The train rumbled forward, streaks of colour flashing past the windows.

Over the roar of the rails Jack shook his head, bewildered. Slowly, he lowered the gun.

Ria Cullen lifted her face from the cards scattered across her family's table. "I don't understand," she whispered.

Jane turned to her. Her pupils had dilated as she inhaled the last of Poppy's soul; now they shrunk again, vapid. "I am she who remains at the end of all," she said quietly. "I go where people are ended, and I collect them. I cannot *be* collected, nor will I ever… *stop*… collecting. I am all there is, in the end. I am what you will give in to."

Cullen shook her head. "No, I understand all that," she sobbed. "I don't understand… why you're on this train."

Jane smiled. Her lips parted. And carefully, gently, she said: "You w—"

The carriage crumpled around them.

The 13:35 to Omaha barrelled toward them, pumping smoke and steam into the air as it thundered down the rails in the wrong direction, both engines screaming toward each other at incredible speed, neither one able to slow down in time, two unstoppable forces spilling soot into the desert as they lunged forward.

There was an incredible screech of metal as the engines smashed into each other, an explosion of hot orange flame balling into a fist and thrusting violently up into the soot-cloud. Steel sheared the sand as both trains crashed off the rails, screaming past each other in a horrendous grinding mess of black and red and white. One ripped the other in half and enormous clouds of glass sprayed the dirt, the rails buckling as candied daylight danced over the carnage. Time seemed to stretch thing around the collision like the two engines had created some impossible vortex: the awful, screeching seconds that followed stretched into minutes, and those into eternities, as each train punched a hole in the other and the two became a twisted, single mass of death and fire.

Eventually, everything was still. The rails smouldered as the husks of both trains lay smashed into sheets of metal and wood in the dirt, still smoking.

Slowly something moved through the wreckage, silent and wraith-like as it bent beneath seats and danced softly down the aisles. It was kind as it touched them, drinking only what it could bear to take, respectfully sidestepping the blood that spilled into the carpet as it swelled and bent like water.

Thick, black fog rose inside the carriages and

pressed against the windows, the entire train filling with shadow. And then, just as quickly as it had swelled, the fog disappeared.

GORGON'S ROCK

Moonlight slithered across the back of the old dead beast, pooling over curved metal and shattering into fragments about the punctures and wounds and great ragged black holes that wracked the thing's spine. White spangles glittered off the mangled, rusted prongs of steel that jutted from its stomach; rivulets of blue ran through the piping of the engine's livery, once painted a bright, glossy green.

The machine had been lying in ruin for decades on an unused siding, its carcass enjoyed by the rats and nocturnal creatures that made their burrows in the abandoned Crowe Hill works. A great leviathan of steam engineering, twisted and ripped apart by the crash and finally, fully slain by almost a century of neglect.

There was something beautiful about it: when

it was alive, the eighteen-wheeled tender engine had been a powerhouse of fiery coal and thick, black smoke, a ruthless steam-powered weapon knifing loudly along the rails. Now it was a gargantuan husk of bent, ruined steel, a shell of a thing plated with moss and chalk. It was still coupled to its train, two once-regal carriages that had followed it willingly to the grave. Many of the windows were smashed, their frames either empty or clinging to the sharp chunks of glass that remained fused to the sealant. The carriages were battered, dented, and a hole in the roof of one had been nested in.

The moonlight that crawled across the dark plates of the wreck was not enough to wake it, but the beast was not dead, not entirely. And as it slept on the siding, banks of chilled air shifted and writhed inside its empty carriages as though pushed by dozens of bodies, moving restlessly between the ragged old seats.

Jo ducked carefully beneath a ropy mess of barbed wire, the cutters still gripped tightly in her hand. The knees of her jeans were soaked through, the gravel beneath her swampy and thick with weeds and hunks of clay. Her backpack snagged on the barbs as she crawled beneath them and she grunted frustratedly, twisting an arm behind her back to yank the bag free.

"Damn," she hissed as she scrambled to her feet inside the fence, slipping the wire cutters back into the side pocket of her backpack and using her already-filthy hands to wipe down her jeans. She was caked in mud and her dark hair was a tangled, frizzy mess of knots, the back of her neck scratched and bleeding where barbs had dug into her flesh. Rubbing her hands together to relieve them of the cold, she shook her whole body and braced herself. When she exhaled, the air before her lips bloomed with a thick, white mist. "The things I do for minimum wage."

Around her, tall square silhouettes lurched out of the trees. Over the last few decades the woodland had been allowed to spread and infest the edges of the old abandoned steam-works, and now the thick and laden branches of aspen and beech trees thrust up around the ruined buildings and punched through their slanted rooves like gnarled, bony claws, bent and pushed by the wind.

An ancient floodlight across the lot flickered, the amber triangle that exploded from it dying and reigniting multiple times a second; the shapes of the buildings around her seemed to swell and wane in the constantly-changing light.

Jo slipped off her backpack and unzipped it, turning her head to look back as she rummaged inside. A thick, black parka rustled as she moved; she imagined she had torn it, crawling through the barbed wire. Outside the fence a winding, moonlit road bent through the trees, and her car – parked half on the verge at the edge of the tarmac – sat dark and lifeless. Way out in the distance a smattering of lights betrayed the location of the village, about three and a half miles from here.

She found what she was looking for and withdrew it from the bag, her fingers curled around the soft, rubbery grip of her camera. Swinging the backpack over her shoulder, she removed the lens cap and looped the strap of the bulky machine around her neck. The Nikon D6 was potentially the most expensive thing she owned – she never would have been able to afford it on her salary, but her father had left her a little over eighteen-thousand pounds in his will with the stipulation that she 'invest in her career' with it – and she had made sure to spend the extra for insurance, too.

Breathing out another puff of white mist, Jo raised the Nikon's viewfinder to her eye and pressed the shutter. A dozen frantic clicks sputtered from the thing's casing and she paused to glance down at the screen and inspect the photographs; quickly she adjusted the ISO settings and took another burst. Satisfied, she pressed on.

Jo crept along the rails toward a squat, leaning water tower, a skeleton of a thing that lurched out of the thick knot of trees which had grown up it and begun to push it over. Its belly was a strip of rusted brown, a dark gash down its side left over from every cascade of rain that spilled off the lid and dribbled down into the gravel. The young woman took a few photos of an old and rotten turntable, half a dozen iron tracks snaking into its maw and another half-dozen snaking, chewed-up and bent, out of it.

As she moved she dug inside her parka for a flashlight and swung a thin beam of light across the ruins, scaring off a small pack of rats that had been following her since the fence; the decayed corpse of a small deer lay across one of the tracks, colourful fungus blooming across its flank and tumbling like soft, clay-red rubble into the cracks of the old, damp sleepers beneath. She snapped another photograph; the editor likely wouldn't put that one in her article, but she found a strange and eerie beauty in the ribbons of colour sprouting from the poor bag of mange.

"Right," she muttered to herself, casting the torchlight in the direction of the looming silhouette on a siding to her left. "Let's take a look at you, shall we?"

Jo shuddered as she crossed the rails toward the old train wreck. Tucking a thick knot of hair behind her ear she glanced about, trying to imagine workmen and drivers bustling about the place, polishing narrow-gauge engines and laughing among themselves. Smoking cigars, probably. This place hadn't been used since the eighties, and even then she found it difficult to imagine the works as a busy hive of activity.

Now, in the moonlit dark and the cold with the gravel crunching too-loud beneath her feet, all she could imagine was some tall, gangly guard in dark uniform erupting suddenly from one of the buildings around her. *What the bluddyell are ya doin ere?* he'd rasp.

Confidently she would flash some kind of identification card, probably one hanging around her neck, and say "Didn't you hear? I'm doing a piece for a very prestigious paper, you've probably heard of us…"

Sighing grimly, she stepped into the shadow of the sleeping Gorgon and held the viewfinder to her eye. The *Haunted Norfolk* magazine was hardly prestigious – hardly a paper – and she doubted very much that their budget could stretch to a lanyard. Oh, *wouldn't* Daddy be proud of what she'd become?

She couldn't help but stare in awe at the old engine, a great dark monster leering up from its buffers. Its funnel was bent, the smokebox beneath caved in, and thick tangles of ivy had snaked up from the rails and slithered into its cab, poking out through various holes in the engine's body. The first few wheels on its left were ground down to a glinting, metallic pulp from where it had sunk onto the rails and screamed off the edge of the cliff; its undercarriage spilled sharp dark shapes onto the gravel beneath where it had exploded on the way down.

Seven passengers in the first-class carriage and thirty-six in second. Plus the driver and fireman, of course, in the cab.

Forty-five lives tumbling off the shredded rails as the engine lunged forward in a shower of sparks, crashing through the buffer-stop and the safety rails, hurtling at a hundred-and-five miles per hour into the canyon below. Forty-five dead. And the Gorgon itself, of course.

Jo moved around the engine, taking photographs from every angle. One of the cab, more fungus spilling across the hard, broken floor; one of the funnel and dome, two equally-broken brothers resting forever on the back of the beast; one of the face of the thing, split in half.

Upon its side the engine's name had been written in a crisp, gold legend. In the last few months somebody had graffitied the livery with a bright, yellow spray paint, cruelly turning the dead thing's name into a terrible, childish pun. Altogether, the words read *GorgonS ROCK*.

It made for a good photograph.

Silently she moved toward the first carriage,

stuffing her cold hands into the pockets of her coat. The Nikon swung lazily against her chest, bouncing with every step. She couldn't help but think of her father as she gazed up at the coaches: another unfortunate passenger on the train of life, a train that was eternally destined to scream off one cliff or another; his had been a heart condition and a fatal error in his paperwork.

The surgery had been scheduled for a date six months after he was due to die. Months of phone calls, e-mails, personal visits to the hospital. Screaming matches with her mother, of which she was not proud; with the nurses, of which she was even less so; and with her father, of which she would forever be mortally ashamed. He had given up fighting by the time the surgery date was finally brought forward; by then, it was far too late.

His train had tumbled quietly, gasping, off the rails at Heart Attack Bluff in the middle of the night, three days before he was scheduled for theatre.

Jo stepped up into the darkness of the first-class coach, passing through a ruptured cavity in the wall and ducking beneath a thick hanging clump of ivy. She raised the camera, photographing the interior of the carriage, then lowered it again and looked calmly around. The windows were small and greasy, smeared with dust, the seats arranged in banks of four: two facing two, with a smart, brass-edged table between them. One of the table supports had bent in and the surface had crashed down into the floor. Cobwebs hung shivering in the corners. At the far end of the narrow aisle, a tall, thin door stood in a wall pocked with holes. Through a tiny glass panel in the door she saw that the adjoining door of the next carriage had been ripped from its frame, and the slender black pit beckoned her grimly forward.

A rat scuttled away somewhere as she moved between the seats, gripping the camera with both hands. She shuddered as a blast of cold air passed through her, instinctively turning her head to look back. Shadows flitted across the walls of the old carriage but nothing moved; nothing but the swaying clutter of ivy in the doorway. Moonlight slid in through the windows and alighted on banks of gold piping that had faded exponentially over the years. Jo pushed forward, a thick clot of unease settling comfortably in her stomach.

Something whispered, right in her ear, and she

yelped quietly, her little scream bouncing off the walls. She hadn't been able to make out the words, but the voice had sounded human; not just a riffle of the wind or the echoing sound of another creature skittering about her. She paused, taking a moment to catch her breath. Since stepping onto the carriage she had felt that somebody was watching her, and again couldn't help but picture the lanky guard that she'd imagined before. The carriage would rock on the rails as he stepped up, swinging a torch beam into her eyes and yelling. *Bluddy get off this train right now, ya daft bint!*

"But mine's the next stop," she whispered to herself, smiling weakly. She remembered train journeys to the city with her father, shrinking down into her seat whenever the ticket collector passed so that they could get away with only paying the child rate for her.

She raised the camera again and squinted through the viewfinder.

A shape passed in front of the lens, a pillar of grey smoke that flickered as it drifted across the aisle. Jo cried out, dropping the camera; it swung down and crashed into her ribs as she stumbled back, looking wide-eyed in the direction of the smoke-shape—

Nothing.

Nothing there at all. But for just a moment through the viewfinder she could've sworn there was something – and that that something had a face.

"You're tired," she told herself, and it was true; she hadn't slept much in the last few days, likely due to the looming deadline for the *HN* article that she'd promised them by Friday morning. More likely, however, was that she'd been having the dream again. The relentless beeping of the machines, dozens of them, the whirr of the empty hospital bed as it folded mechanically in on itself and unfolded again, and then the shape behind her, the shadow lurching forward – and then she turned, screaming as she saw her mother coming into the room, not walking but floating on motionless feet, gripping a pair of scissors tightly in her hand, raising them high…

Jo bit her lip, stirring herself. She always awoke before the scissors came down, but she had seen the body in the morgue. The bruised, misshapen welt in her mother's neck where she had buried the twin blades in a moment of utter grief.

"Don't cry," Jo said quietly, stepping forward. "Don't cry, not now, don't cry…"

Scream, whispered a voice in her left ear, and she did.

***

Shadows slithered up the walls of the carriage and crashed together on its ceiling, a sudden gust of air rocking the thing on its siding and tipping Jo back into one of the seats.

"Jesus!" she yelled, stumbling to steady herself. The camera swung like a pendulum from her neck and she stopped it with one hand, gripping the back of the seat with the other. Frantically she whirled around, looking for the bastard who'd hissed into her ear. "Come on, quit playing silly… buggers…"

The carriage was empty.

"What?" she whispered, her eyes darting from seat to seat. Blooms of soft, yellow padding spilled from ripped banks of upholstery, the corduroy piping having burst open – or been torn open – years ago. Dust hung in the air, clouds of it gathering and spreading, moving as though slipping between tiny air currents.

Frowning, Jo focused her attention on a clump of moonlit particles that hung over the broken table, a clump that seemed to swell in size then wane again, swell then wane.

Slowly, she raised the camera and looked through the viewfinder.

Right behind the convulsing cloud stood a translucent grey clot of mist in the shape of a woman, the table slicing her neatly in half. Her eyes were bright white points, blazing furiously like flashlight reflections in silver. Her jaw hung slack, her form at once ethereally ambiguous and horribly, definitively skeletal.

Jo screamed again, whirling around, still peering through the viewfinder when the lens swung toward the rip in the side of the carriage through which she'd entered. There, another grey shape crouched in the aisle, a young man with the same bright, flat discs buried in the eye-sockets of his skull. "No," Jo moaned, swinging the camera across the train. Three smoky figures sat in a booth on the left, their brilliant white eyes pointed in her direction, their bone-white faces still and emotionless. "No, no…"

She dropped the camera and backed up,

bumping the seat behind her with her hip. Another explosion of cool air smacked her in the chest and she tipped backward as the carriage rocked again, grabbing for something to keep her from landing on her rump.

Her head swam, blood pounding in her ears. She snapped her head left and right, looking for signs of life, but there was nothing in the empty carriage, nothing but the oddly-pulsating clouds of dust and the insects that skittered across the walls.

Then something pushed her.

She felt the hands on her chest, slamming so powerfully into her that she knew immediately a bruise would form; she was launched backward, tripping over her own feet and landing against the door at the very back of the carriage. Instinctively she grabbed the handle and rattled it, glancing anxiously behind her as the hairs on her neck stood on end and her blood ran cold as ice.

Half a dozen disembodied pairs of white points glared at her from the seats.

Jo yelled as the door burst open suddenly, swinging out from beneath her. She crashed out of the carriage and lurched forward, her leg twisting around the couplings connecting the two coaches;

she fell like lead, her head smacking a thick metal plate. A knot of warmth spread from the base of her skull and the *clang!* resounded, her whole body convulsing as an electric bolt of agony shot down her spine.

She lay there for a moment, her leg throbbing hard, her head swimming. Heavy ragged breaths ripped through her body, chest heaving. Slowly she heaved herself into a sitting position among the thick cables of the coupling, her legs twisted up, the toes of one boot scraping the sleeper beneath. Tiny glass shards tinkled as they rolled off her parka. She glanced down and saw that the camera lens had shattered.

"Fuck," she whispered. Images of her father smashed through her aching skull and a pang of guilt knifed her stomach. She thought: *at least I'll have plenty to write about for that* Haunted *article.*

And with that thought, remembered exactly what had led her to tumble out of the carriage. She looked up, wide-eyed, and her mouth opened in a long, low groan.

A huddle of well-dressed passengers stood in the doorway, looking down at her. They were all oddly well-dressed, smart old-fashioned shirts and waistcoats emblazoned with gold embroidery; hair pinned back or neatly combed; blood everywhere. She recognised one of them instantly: the woman's photograph had been printed with the article about the Gorgon's fateful crash, her face unnervingly calm in black-and-white, her hair white. Some Russian diplomat, Jo remembered.

Cause of death: blunt chest trauma.

The woman with the white hair had been crushed against a table as the train plummeted to its grave. Not a single one of her ribs had been unbroken when they salvaged the bodies from the wreck; both lungs were punctured.

She was as dead as they come.

"This isn't happening," Jo moaned. "Oh, god, this isn't…"

One of them – a young girl with blinding white eyes and a pretty yellow summer dress – smiled awfully, her teeth flashing in the moonlight. "Hello," she whispered.

"Jesus!" Jo yelled and scrambled back, her eyes snapping from face to face as the dead stared blankly back at her. Crawling, grabbing, she staggered to her feet and almost fell back into the second carriage through the open doorway. "Jesus, get away from me!"

Stomach in her mouth. Blood cold and thick like ice, some of it running in a thick, wet river down the back of her neck. Jo squeezed her eyes shut to blot out the agony of her throbbing skull and the grainy afterimages of those awful, pale figures burned itself on the back of her eyelids. The pain in her leg was incredible and she wheeled around, flopping into the nearest seat and clutching breathlessly at her bent calf. Just for a moment, she thought, just until—

"You shouldn't be here," said a little voice.

Jo's eyes snapped open.

A young boy sat across the table from her, a thick mop of black curls falling in his eyes. Eyes like bright white discs, flat and cold and piercing. Jo looked from the boy to his mother, perched in the seat beside him, and the woman smiled thinly. Her eyes were the same. Her forehead was all smashed in, the bone wrecked. But she was real – right there in front of Jo's eyes – real and close enough to touch.

"What… where…"

Seven passengers in the first-class carriage and thirty-six in second.

Jo balked, looking out into the aisle.

Every seat was full, every eye on her. No longer movements in the air or pillars of smoke but flesh and blood, as real and vivid as her. All thirty-six of them, dressed in the clothes they'd died in, sitting in the *seats* they'd died in…

"Oh, god," Jo breathed, hauling herself onto her broken ankle and screaming as agony shot up into her hip. As one, every passenger in the carriage stood, backs straight, faces pinned on her as she stood awkwardly and whirled back toward the door.

She burst forward, red hot pain everywhere, grabbing both sides of the frame and tipping forward, desperate to get out, to get away—

She froze, her eyes on the couplings beneath her and the body that lay sprawled among them, one leg twisted in the cables, head tipped back. Impaled on something that she couldn't see, blood pooling over the metal and falling in thick, gluey strings into the gravel below.

She looked from the body to the passengers in the first-class carriage and back again. It couldn't be. No, oh, no, it couldn't be…

Slowly, she reached for her camera and tipped

it forward, glancing down into the blank black screen of the viewfinder.

Two bright white points reflected back at her.

"No," she whispered. "Please…"

She felt a tiny hand slip itself into hers. It felt as real and solid as the hand of something living, but it was cold.

Everything was cold. And all the pain was gone, as though she had never felt it at all.

She looked down, and the boy from the booth looked back up at her. "Come," he said, "sit with us."

Jo swallowed, looking back toward the empty seat at the table. All the passengers had sat back down and seemed to have forgotten about her, returning to each other. Silent conversations rippled on the stale air; a decades-old card game continued between two couples near the back of the carriage, their bodies ruined by various bruises and cuts.

Jo shook her head. "This can't be happening," she whispered.

"It already has," the boy said softly, guiding her to her seat.

Jo looked back at her body one last time and

blinked. She wanted to cry, but nothing came.

Slowly, calmly, she sat down and laid her hands on the table. "Well," she said shakily, hoping desperately that her voice wasn't betraying her terror. "Where does this thing stop?"

TURN

THE

LIGHTS

OFF

AS

YOU

LEAVE

Shannon had only vague recollections of her grandfather's apartment: a burry carousel of images and half-memories, tossed and blended into a kaleidoscopic palette of various browns and greys. She remembered the smell of cigar smoke, most prominent in the cramped living area and especially so near the old oak dresser in one corner, where an ashtray permanently smouldered. She remembered the single cracked tile on the kitchen floor, otherwise a checkerboard of terracotta red and bone white. Details like these seemed to have branded themselves onto that spinning reminiscent drum, a whirling confusion of sounds and smells and rusted brass fittings; Shannon could hardly remember the bathroom at all, or her grandfather's bedroom, but she knew that the bathtub rested on three clawed feet and that a small, thick chopping board propped up the corner where the fourth had broken off, and she knew that Grandpa Brown slept beneath an enormous framed print of Bruegel's *Dulle Griet.*

She could not remember her grandfather's face, though in the days following the news of his death she tried very hard to.

She remembered his hands – knuckles piled carelessly on top of knuckles with such abandon that they clicked and rolled over each other, and long, stiff, fingers stained yellow with Lucky Strike tobacco – and the way the light seemed to change whenever he stepped into a room; he had been a very tall man, and Shannon knew that as a child she had been quite afraid of visiting his grotty little apartment on West Howard, for even when Grandpa Brown stooped, so as not to blot out the gritty phosphorescence of the bare bulbs, they flickered like a dim halo around his hunched shoulders and made him look like some slender, spectral creature from another world.

She moved blindly across the street, coils of rain snapping and dancing about her like millions of razor wires suspended in the air: thin, electric cables lashed with the sizzling colours of the neon lights all around, crisscrossed and perpetually slicing through the dark so that the soaked tarmac flashed black and white. Shannon had stopped in Dunning on her way from the O'Hare International to buy a four-pack for the long evening ahead, and now all four cans of Miller Lite were shoved into the pockets of her coat and she held the plastic carrier bag over her head. It did little to stop the rain from falling into her eyes, but it kept her hair from blowing in her face and, rather more importantly, blotted out some of the noise and the chaos. She had only been to Chicago four times – three of them to visit her grandfather, and once to interview for a post at the *Tribune* that she turned down for something closer to home – and each time it had rained like this, turning every street into a writhing madness of stomping feet and blaring headlights. If she remembered nothing else, she remembered the rain.

The horn of an all-black Buick GNX screamed behind her as she splashed onto the sidewalk and toward the neon-lit lobby of the apartment building. Shannon whipped around to watch it swerve around a pedestrian in a bright red raincoat, the car moving like a slick, oily shadow through the rain. The bodega across the street was a hive of activity, fluorescent lights plastering greasy squares onto the windows. She stood for a moment in the shadow of the tall building behind her and watched as West Howard folded and unfolded, folded and unfolded again: men and women running through lances of sharp, pink rain; children appearing from one doorway and disappearing into another; battered Accords and Escorts fighting through puddles, stopping and starting; windows rolled down, fists shoved out.

Something passed overhead. Something invisible in the rain and the dark, a huge, heavy shape that moved by painting shadows on the walls, which it hastily peeled away as it thundered wraith-like toward South Boulevard. The sidewalk trembled, the cement rumbling as though something had burrowed beneath her through layers of earth and silt. Only when the terrible shadow had disappeared did she realise that she'd closed her eyes; opening them cautiously, Shannon lowered the carrier bag from above her head and stepped back toward the lobby.

She didn't look up as she raised the pad of her thumb to the buzzer beside the wide glass door.

She pressed in one of the scratched, steel buttons with a soft *click* and cringed in response to the strangled thrill that followed. She waited, tucking her hands into her pockets as the next moment stretched into something unbearable, something that she knew might snap back into itself if it were only pulled a little tighter—

A grunt crackled through the speaker in the shape of a pair of words Shannon couldn't hope to make out, and she bustled closer to the panel to reply. "I'm sorry it's so late," she said, "I've come to collect a few things from number eighteen? I think my mother spoke to you yesterday…"

Another dull buzz, a *clunk*, and the glass door opened lazily, barely nudged out of its frame.

"Thank you," she murmured into the buzzer panel, but the woman in seventeen had already left. Shannon crumpled the drenched carrier bag in one hand, tossed it into a tall, stainless steel trash can on the corner of the sidewalk, and pulled the door all the way open to step inside and out of the rain.

She moved hurriedly across the lobby toward a narrow elevator at the back of the building.

Quickly she leant forward to jab the button and call it down, her jacket swinging with the weight of the cans inside. A soft bell rang somewhere distant as the elevator began to thunder down the shaft behind the wall, and she stepped back to glance about the lobby of the building. The walls were plain and slathered with whorls of pale, crumbling plaster, the floor carpeted with a thick, white shag that had been quite horribly ruined: damp, slarry trails of brown created a wet swamp from the door to the staircase on her left, and gritty black footprints made a patchwork of stains in the middle of the hall. Two electric lanterns hung on the wall across from the staircase, flickering like gas lamps; a third was bracketed to the banister, and from somewhere on the next floor a fourth cast its light onto the stairs.

Another bell, and she returned her attention to the elevator as the doors slid open with a shudder. Like the mandibles of some horrid, hungry maw, the doors peeled back to reveal the great black throat of the elevator. Shannon stepped back instinctively.

It was dark inside. The flickering light of the lobby brushed the edges of the elevator – enough for her to discern that she was indeed looking into the elevator carriage itself, and not simply an empty shaft – but everything beyond those fortunate first few inches was sunk back into complete blackness. A circuit must have broken inside the elevator, for even the control panel was unlit. The floor was a deep pool of inky shadow, and the walls seemed to have fallen away so that the chamber could have stretched for miles into a void of absolute pitch.

"Nope," Shannon muttered, turning away from the hell-black elevator and moving to the staircase without looking back.

She climbed quickly, running her hands through her soaked hair to remove it from her face. Her pant legs were drenched and clung to her calves, thick and cool and dripping onto the stairs. With one hand on the banister rail she came out on a narrow hallway and crossed it hastily to reach the next staircase, narrower than the first and sandwiched against the wall. Nearby, three doors in varnished pine led to apartments two, three, and four. Another seemed to lead to a janitor's closet of some sort, for it had a hazardous red skull slapped into a triangle upon it. The apartments must have been very small, she surmised, or at least very cleverly packed into the fabric of the building, for the doors to apartments two and three stood abreast and right in the corner, leaving four alone at the far end of the hall. She saw, around a dim corner, another set of elevator doors, and almost shuddered at the thought.

She had reached the third floor before she felt *it* again.

This time the rumble of something crashing through the darkness alongside the outer wall of the house was amplified, and yet thinned by something in the makeup of the building: it became a rattle, and an almost skeletal one at that, though it was far louder than any crash of bone Shannon could imagine. The thundering movement of the thing outside reverberated through the flickering husk of the building with such ferocity that the iron banister in her hand physically shook; the stairs at her feet juddered so violently she thought they might split open. And then it was gone, again, that awful rattling thing carrying itself off into the night. Echoes ran down the steel rods in the walls: the beastly, monstrous snake may have slithered off, but it had sloughed off its skin and left it all over.

She continued on to the fourth floor, where the door for apartment ten hung wide open. The doors for eight and nine stood close to each other – ten alone on the right, so that the arrangement of the apartments seemed opposite to that of those on the lower levels – and a deep well of darkness pooled behind the open door. She tried to peer inside, hoping to see some sign of life, but she only glimpsed the corner of a shadowy desk, covered in papers that fluttered in the draft through what she presumed must be an open window. The hallway light flickered.

Shannon found apartment eighteen on the seventh floor.

Standing at the top of the stairs, she glanced across the hall toward the elevator doors and saw that they were open. Frowning, she stepped forward, opening her mouth to call out. The elevator was dark, barely illuminated by the light of the hall itself, a deep tunnel of black that seemed as though it might sink right out of the building and into the street beyond. But she hadn't heard the elevator moving since calling it to the first floor… she didn't suppose she would have, though, with the penetrating smack of rain on the walls and the sound of her own blood pounding in her ears.

A feeble bell chimed suddenly, yanking her heart up into her mouth where it pounded against her jaw. The elevator doors slammed shut all too quickly, crashing into one another and sealing away the dark beyond. Then came a rumble, not unlike the thundering roll of the thing outside, and the elevator began to drop into the belly of the building.

Forcing her mouth closed and gritting her teeth quite consciously, Shannon returned her attention to the door of apartment eighteen. She fumbled in her coat for the keys her mother had mailed to her and her knuckles bounced awkwardly off the aluminium can in her pocket, the metal slick with condensation. Finding the keys and hooking them into her fingers, she took one last look at the elevator before steeling herself and heading purposefully for the door.

A thick, dry *snap!* like the gnarled roots of an old tree twisting free.

The hallway light above her blinked out, right above her head, and she was plunged into darkness.

Her head tipped back and she saw the wire coil in the bulb sizzle orange before blackening completely, and then the pitch of the hallway swallowed her whole. She froze, her chest tightening, the keys suddenly very cold in her hand.

There was a cough from inside apartment seventeen, and a voice – one she recognised from the buzzer at the lobby door – that said, quite simply, "It does that."

"The light?" Shannon asked after a moment. She recoiled, almost ashamed of the timidity of her own voice.

"Switch is by the stairs, love," the woman in seventeen grunted.

Shannon turned her head, moving slowly. Cautiously. Almost heard the bones of her neck grinding against each other like stone on stone. She saw the switch, its pale face illuminated barely by the seeping light of the floor below, a light that limped and dragged itself up the stairs but stopped there, came no further. "Thank you," Shannon called, and she hurried across the hall.

The lights came on with a soft *clock*, nothing like the breaking of dry bone that had shut them off. Glassy, yellow light filled the hallway, almost blinding after the sudden and consuming dark. She pressed across the awful shag carpet toward apartment eighteen without looking up at the bulb, her face twisted into a stony grimace. She had never liked the dark. She was not one of those frail, childish people who were afraid of it, but she certainly would have preferred to know that she was safe, and in her own home, if the lights were going to suddenly suffocate themselves like that.

And after all, she thought as she fumbled with the key in the lock of the door to apartment eighteen, it could not be the dark itself that she was afraid of, for that dark was a perfectly natural occurrence – was, in fact, the natural state of all things, and would still cover most of them, most of the time, had the lightbulb never been invented – no, it was the things that might have lived and moved and breathed *inside* the dark that she was afraid of.

"Not afraid," she whispered as the lock clicked and the door was shunted gently open. "Just reasonably wary."

But she was afraid, in this moment. For when she had turned to look in the direction of the light switch, she had seen something. And she wondered, now, whether it was grief or exhaustion or just plain insanity that had forced such a vision upon her, but a part of her couldn't help but think that… well, that she had simply seen what had actually been there. That there really *might* be things living in the spaces the light never reached.

Just for a second, in the thick, black dark at the top of the stairs, she had seen a pair of silvery points that had looked for all the world like two wickedly glinting eyes.

Absolute dark.

The door swung shut behind her and Shannon's breath hitched in her throat as a stale wave of air blew her forward into the cramped, blacked-out space. The ripe smell of old salami hit her instantly, followed by a waft of cigarette smoke. It was a good five or six degrees cooler in the apartment than it had been in the hall; she shivered, overcome with the cloying closeness of the air and the walls.

"All right," she whispered, fumbling around the doorframe, "if I were a decrepit old alcoholic, where would *I* hide the—"

The air exploded with sound and the building shuddered as an enormous weight seemed to crash into the wall outside. A narrow window at the edge of Shannon's vision flared up with greasy yellow light as the rumbling leviathan outside screamed past the apartment, shaking the ground beneath her feet. She almost buckled as the thing roared, the low bellow of a foghorn blaring and making the window rattle in its frame. Her head whipped round as mad splashes of light cascaded up the walls around her.

She screamed.

A shape lurched toward her, crumpling under its own weight as it launched itself from the wall just three feet from where she stood. Tall, taller than any man, and bundled in strips of filthy leather that flowed and rippled in the lights crashing past the window. A creature of immense proportion with a tangled nest of legs and feet knotted beneath it. The thing ripped itself from the wall, tossing the shadows with it, reaching for her—

The rumbling faded as the leviathan outside disappeared into the night, and with it the swinging straps of leather became still.

Where the monster had been, in the dim afterglow of the yellow lights, a thick pouch of jackets and scarves hung from the wall. Beneath, Grandpa Brown's shoes were piled up by the door like the collection of some worn leather-obsessed kleptomaniac, a mound of stubbed toes and scuffed suede. The creature's flailing legs and arms were mere shadows, pressed back against the plaster. Her heart still pounding, Shannon bent forward to fumble within the hanging mound of dirty coats, and her fingers found the light switch. She jabbed it and winced as the hallway light came on above her. Glancing up, she saw that her grandfather had never bothered to dress the light with a shade; the bulb hung bare and sizzling from a thick, black cable anchored in the raw, cracked mess of the ceiling, the filament buzzing softly.

Briefly embarrassed by her fear, Shannon waited to see if the woman in the apartment next door had noticed her screaming. After a few moments' silence, she supposed the roar of the leviathan outside must have blotted it out.

Gingerly, she moved into the cramped den area, crossing a sparse few feet of ratty carpet before stepping over the threshold. Her grandfather's belongings were scattered everywhere, untouched. A low, corduroy armchair was stained with beer and coffee, and grubby yellow handprints on the arms showed her just how hard Grandpa Brown had crunched his bony fingers into the material as he sat watching the old twelve-inch Ferguson across the room. Heaps of newspaper clippings lay across a scratched, pine coffee table and glossy pools of paste had congealed in the carpet to make a trail from the sitting area to the narrow window at the end of the room.

A part of her was surprised that the police investigation hadn't more thoroughly disturbed the carefully-curated mess of the old man's apartment, but she supposed there had been very little for them to investigate. Inside the apartment, at least; most of Grandpa Brown had been spattered on the wall *out*side. She tried to imagine how they'd possibly been able to scrape him off; then she tried desperately not to.

Shannon bent forward to set her cans upon the coffee table, drawing each one from her coat with a growing sense of unease. Above her, another bare bulb flickered, then stilled. Soft light oozed down the walls, pale blue paper curling into husks and scraps and revealing the crumbling brickwork beneath. She lined up three of the cans, each half an inch from the last, logos facing the wall. Standing straight, she popped open the fourth and drank quickly, foam hissing over her lower lip. The beer was warm. She drained half a can and set it with the others, pausing to line it up properly before crossing the room past a burned stove and a tiny, glass-fronted refrigerator in one corner.

The dark had never frightened her when she was a child – and that was not to say that it did now, but she did at least understand that there was a certain comfort to be found in the presence of light. She knew that some of the other kids were afraid, and in a way she could understand why, but her mother had always told her that it was just like everything else you were supposed to be scared of: like so many of those other things – like spiders, and snakes, and rats – it could be killed. And killing the dark was as simple as turning the lights on. All it took was a *click*.

And then her mother had started drinking.

Shannon's father had left, and taken most of their savings with him, but Mother had found a sum of money that, along with a string of poorly-concealed one night stands with their landlord, managed to keep the bathroom cupboard stocked with enough rum to topple a large bull, and kept a tab with the Old Maid as though the kegs had been consistently diluted with water from the fountain of youth itself.

Shannon had heard the stories about Grandpa Brown's 'black days' – the period of his life that the old man could barely remember, and that Shannon's mother tried so dearly not to – and tried to confront the woman, but by then it was too late.

Even now, fresh out of an AA rehabilitation scheme so vigorous that she seemed to rely on quotes from the Big Book every time she crafted a sentence, Shannon's mother still seemed to be on the edge of the pit that she'd fallen into: standing over it like she was waiting for something to come up and pull her in, rather than simply waiting to fall.

Mother's days had never been so black as her Grandpa Brown's, but she had come close. And now Shannon was afraid – *not afraid, just...suspicious* – of the dark, like she should have been when she was a child. And as much as she had forgiven her mother for what had happened, she didn't think she would ever forget.

She stood by the window of Grandpa Brown's den and looked out onto the street. Neon lights washed in from the left, painting the rain in shades of green and purple as the wind whipped it into a blazing frenzy. Just below the window, a rusted fire escape ran down to the sidewalk, spiralling in on itself and rutting into the wall of the building. Shannon had to squint, but after a moment or two she saw it: barely twelve inches from the safety rail, the monorail track drew long, black scars through the rain, a sheer cliff of iron shafts that veered blindly down the street and dragged great wide sheets of water with them, curtains of dripping white that blasted the tarmac beneath.

Just something you get used to, her mother had always said. Living this close to the L was like living in their old New England house with the groaning pipes: the frequent rumble and rattle of the passing trains on the elevated line was terrifying the first few times, but then it just faded into the background like everything else.

Maybe that was why Grandpa Brown had stepped off the fire escape and onto the tracks.

Not to go out in a ripping, sucking implosion of

blood and tissue, but to fade into the background…
like everything else.

Just something you get used to, she thought, and
she turned away from the window and returned to
the coffee table.

She withdrew the list from her jeans pocket,
wincing as damp ribbons of paper smeared her
fingers. Her mother had faxed the instructions to
her from her real estate offices in Hampshire;
Shannon didn't know why they couldn't have just
discussed it over the phone, but there was
something comforting about the older woman's
compact, flowing scribble:

vinyl collection (just the good ones)

Shannon drained the rest of the first Miller Lite
and popped open a second before folding the list
back into her pocket. Glancing around the tiny den,
she saw a battered portable record player on a
squat dresser by the bedroom door. The dresser's
glass door was hanging open and it was empty
inside, a thick carpet of dust covering the shelves.

She swore.

"But if *I* were a lanky drunken prick…" she whispered, still holding the can as she moved to the bedroom and crossed the threshold. She reached around for the light switch with her free hand and flicked it on, flooding the miniature space with a dim wash of amber. She could barely step any farther into the room: the single bed filled most of it, leaving only a narrow alleyway along one wall. Grandpa Brown's clothes were tossed into piles on the floor, some spilling out of the drawers of a scorched bedside cabinet. Briefly setting the beer can down on the floor, she reached forward, grimacing with disgust as she swiped at the lamp on the bedside cabinet and clumsily screwed the bulb into place. It warmed instantly, almost burning her hands, and a second pool of light spread into the room.

A dark shroud still hung over the bed. The print that she remembered so vividly from her childhood visits had been slapped into a dull black frame onto the wall: a bad copy of a nightmare painting; an insane, hellish landscape that only a madman could sleep beneath. Shadows rolled down the walls and uncurled clawed fingers over the edges of the mattress.

She tried not to look, to think about the last time her grandfather had been in this room – had slept in this bed – but it was impossible not to. The chewed duvet was still thrown into the corner of the mattress as though he'd only rolled out of it moments ago; the mattress itself was stained with various swilling patterns of brown and grey where he'd relieved himself; the pillow was deflated and sprayed with clots of blood and matted white hair. "Oh, god," she moaned, raising a hand to her mouth. She imagined him bending out of the mattress, his broken body folding over itself as his knuckles and bony knees clicked into motion, limbs extending spider-like, imagined him crawling drunkenly through the mess of the bedroom into the den – and then to the window…

She stumbled back, kicking the can she'd left by the door. It tipped over and foamed across the carpet, crackling as the bubbles popped and a thin, honey-coloured liquid seeped into the froth.

"Shit," Shannon muttered, wheeling around to pick up the tin. Her rump hit the edge of the bed as she squatted and pain rocked up her hip. She grabbed the empty can and looked around desperately for something to clean up the spreading puddle. "Shit, shit…"

Her eyes fell upon the dark space beneath the bed. Two silvery points of light blinked up at her. Something shot out of the dark. A pair of hands thrust toward her – hands with long, bony fingers, knuckles piled on top of knuckles, the skin so pale it was almost translucent – the arms impossibly long and *stretching*—

She blinked, and the image disappeared.

Poking out from beneath the lip of the mattress was her grandfather's record collection.

Two dozen or so vinyl discs in faded sleeves, the corners of which had been chewed and mashed by mice. She reached hesitantly for the small stack and dragged the records awkwardly from beneath the bed, the spilled beer forgotten. She gathered them into her arms and stood, moving back into the den and dumping them on the coffee table.

For a moment she stood staring at the yellowed handprints on the armchair beside her. In her mind she saw them again, those terrible, long hands reaching out from the dark. Knuckles popping and rattling as they rolled over each other. The arms bent and clicked, stretching, unravelling within the sleeves of a long, brown coat, the material frayed and worn, the skin bone-white and whispering…

Only the good ones.

Her mother would appreciate Sinatra's greatest hits and Robert Johnson's *King of the Delta Blues Singers*, but Shannon doubted there'd be much love for Tom Jones or The McCoys. She put aside the single Springsteen album for herself, and went to return the rest to the bedroom.

The lights flickered as she crossed the threshold of the tiny room, a dim whistle building all around her as the walls were splashed with erratic patches of yellow and amber. The whistle built to a whine and she whirled around, looking back toward the front door. The bare bulb above Grandpa Brown's shoes was flickering too. For almost a full minute the fluttering grew in intensity, the whining now a steady, electric weeping; sparks seemed to explode from the filaments and she thought that whatever mad storm of energy was rushing the bulbs might just blow them all completely—

For a fraction of a second, the apartment was entirely dark. She heard the scuttling of an insect – no, the rapping of bony fingers on plaster – then silence. The lights came back on; the flickering had stopped. Light swelled and waned slowly on the walls, the dim glow of each bulb less steady than before but certainly not flashing so blindly as moments ago. Streams of yellow peeled up the paper and shifted, almost swaying like weeds underwater.

Unnerved by the bony scuttling sound, Shannon reached down and shoved the rest of her grandfather's vinyls under the bed. She left the bedroom hastily, wincing as the frothing carpet squelched beneath her boot heel.

The L roared again outside the window as she unfolded the crumpled list from her pocket. A mechanical snake of bulging carriages rattled past the window, shockingly fast, squares of light screaming past the window and blurring into an endless river of glassy lightning. She hardly noticed the rumble of wheels, the pneumatic hiss and whine of the gangway bellows compressing and stretching, accordion-like; she read quickly and tucked the note back into her jeans.

jewelry (in bathtub?)

Shannon frowned, glancing up and across the

den. The bathroom door was closed, the ash scarred and warped and stained so that she could imagine a long, moaning face in the knotted wood. She approached carefully, her eyes skirting the frame in an attempt to discern any light bleeding through from the other side; there was none, only a thin slit of black all the way around. That seemed dreadful, for some reason – there was no reason that a light would have been left on in there, of course, but something about the dark behind a closed door was always somehow worse than the dark of a room you were already in – and she laid her fingers on the handle with some trepidation.

She pushed, and the darkness yawned out into the den before sinking back and letting a thin wash of light inside. The tiles on the floor were cracked, smashed to pieces; she had remembered the single broken tile from years ago, alone in its damage and surrounded by pristine squares of red and white, but now it was all splintered, a great mosaic of broken teeth and gums mashed into a surface that could hardly be called flat anymore. She reached around the doorframe and tugged on a thin, frayed cord; the bathroom was flooded with light—

And then it wasn't.

There was a dull *snap* and the apartment seemed to shudder as it slipped into darkness again. The bathroom light went first, the bulb dying with such a loud suddenness that she jumped; the den light snapped off next, something popping behind her and forcing her to turn around on instinct – just in time to see the bedroom light do the same. Her head wheeled toward the front door and the hallway light sizzled, flashed orange, then died like the others.

Alone in the pitch, she drew in a long, ragged breath and held it. Above her head, that scuttling sound again: long legs

(*fingers*)

drumming on the plaster as some creature retreated into the dark, dark den. She was suddenly very small, surrounded by suffocating clouds of black and entirely blind.

"Christ," she murmured, letting out her breath and fumbling for the cord. She tugged it sharply and the bathroom light came on again. She stood in a tiny square of light, looking out on the apartment as a weak glow rolled over the carpet around her; not enough to see all the way across the den, but she remembered her way to the switch well enough.

She turned on the den light first, then stepped back into the bedroom, moving carefully around the spilled can of Miller Lite and leaning for the switch. She flicked it on and considered screwing the bulb of the bedside lamp in, too, but quickly realised the bulb must have blown completely; after all, it couldn't have unscrewed itself. Moving back to the cramped hallway, she reached again into the coats hanging from the wall and turned on the final switch, flooding the rest of the apartment with the greasy glow of the last, dirty lightbulb.

Running a hand through her hair, Shannon headed back to the bathroom, making a quick detour to pop the tab of the third beer can. She took a quick slug and placed it down again, suddenly feeling as though there might be something watching her.

Something in the apartment with her.

Shaking off the uneasy feeling, she stepped into the bathroom and looked down at the tub. She half-smiled at the sight of the stubby chopping board propping up one corner of the ancient ceramic-encased thing, exactly where she remembered it. The other three feet were like little clawed brass fists, each clutched oppressively around a tiny secret. The tub was enormous, considering the meagre size of the bathroom, and its curved rim folded in on itself to create a neat bevel around the edge.

Wincing as she knelt down on the tiles, Shannon reached up into the bevelled rim of the tub and fumbled blindly in the tiny, narrow space. She almost expected to find nothing at all, but before too long her fingers had settled on a long, lumpen shape pressed to the ceramic beneath a layer of ribbed duct tape.

"Absolute fucking headcase," she whispered, grunting as she ripped off the tape with some resistance. It peeled away with a dreadful sucking sound and something clinked gently to the grotty floor beneath the tub. Reaching down with her free hand, she grasped for the necklace and plucked it out of the dust. It was sticky with residual paste-like adhesive and she scrunched up her face in disgust, wondering how many earrings and bangles she'd have to peel from their hiding places. "Why couldn't you just keep a jewellery case like anybody else?"

She worked her hands around the edge of the

tub for a good five minutes, tearing off ragged strips of duct tape and retrieving the grubby rings and gemstones that had been affixed there. She filled her jacket with jewellery and, finally, stood up, moving to the scale-caked washbasin to rinse her hands of all the dust and spiderweb that had stuck to them. She ran the tap and looked up into the mirror, breathing slowly to calm herself.

Her hair was still soaked and hung down to her shoulders past a face that looked almost white in the dreadful half-light. Her eyes were dull, lips colourless, cheeks sallow. She had been working so hard for the last few months that she'd barely taken the time to look after herself – look *after* herself – and looking now, she was almost shocked to see just how thin her neck had become, swallowed entirely by her blouse and the damp collar of her coat. And how many articles of hers had actually been picked up? Was it worth all the sleepless nights and long, gradually-chipping-away days?

She was almost thankful, for a moment, that her grandfather had passed; at least she had finally stepped away from the typewriter for a moment.

A shadow flitted past her, slipping across the

glass of the mirror like a wraith, and it took her a moment to realise that it was not, after all, something moving inside the apartment, but the lights flickering again; another brief flash of darkness and then the bulbs seemed to settle. Her heart stilled in her chest and she turned slowly, looking out into the den.

She could imagine him sitting there, a stretched, thin man hunched over the newspaper with his scissors – slicing through articles with some insane fervour like a child pressing flowers or holding a magnifying glass to an ants' nest. She could see him moving through the apartment, never opening his mouth, never saying a word to himself, just passing from room to room, turning the lights off as he left each one. That was another thing that she remembered: Grandpa Brown never, not once, allowed more than one of the lights in his apartment to be switched on at once. After all, he'd always said, he couldn't be in more than one *room* at any one time, now, could he?

Shannon's mother had told her that she hadn't always followed that rule as a child, but she had quickly learned. Grandpa Brown had taught her, in his 'black days', just how to make every cent count

– just how much every cent *mattered* – and he had made sure she listened.

From what Shannon understood, he had beat the practice into her.

Turn the lights off as you leave, she imagined him saying, before he snapped the belt into her back. *Turn off every light as you leave.*

Shuddering, she stepped back into the den and burrowed in her pocket for the list. Unfolding it, she headed for the coffee table, already reaching down for another drink—

The lights went off with a *snap!* and the apartment was plunged into darkness again.

Suddenly overcome with anger, Shannon yelled, "They just fucking *do that*, do they?" and ploughed forward. Her shin crashed into the coffee table and she wheeled forward, the note blasted from her hand as her knees smacked the ground. Her head clocked the edge of a little round table beside the sofa and a bright bolt of pain shot through her skull. She heard that scuttling sound again over her head and looked up.

Outside, the headlights of another approaching train exploded through the window. The den walls were splashed with warm flares of lamplight and she gasped as the thing on the ceiling was finally illuminated. The train thundered past and the apartment shook violently, the whole building rattling from top to bottom, but she barely felt it, barely noticed – she was transfixed, her gaze fused to the thing moving across the plaster.

An old, withered hand, knuckles smashed into knuckles, withdrew from the extinguished bulb on the end of a slender, spidery arm that was six or seven times too long. Bony fingers rapped the ceiling as the hand skittered backward, the nails clicking loudly. Then the train had passed by and the light from the window was swallowed by another explosion of darkness, and as the apartment stopped shuddering, Shannon finally let out her breath.

Dismissing the awful image as some figment of her imagination, stimulated by the overwhelming flashes of darkness and her memories of this place, Shannon stood and carefully made her way to the switch. The bulb came on and flickered, buzzing a little. Bending down to retrieve the scrappy paper that had fallen from her hand, she checked the last item on the list:

grandma

Shannon shuddered, crumpling the list into her pocket. Well, at least she knew where her grandmother *was*; she wouldn't have to go fumbling beneath Grandpa Brown's bed or around the edges of his grimy bathtub.

She moved into the hall and stood beneath the dim bulb, squinting into the darkness of that little well of shadow by the door. It was incredible that such a small apartment could not be illuminated by a single bulb, but she supposed the low wattage had something to do with that, along with the thick coat of grease smearing the glass. She almost bumped into the cabinet where Grandma was kept.

Cursing, she crouched to peer into the glass-fronted bureau. The urn was somewhere in there, her grandmother's ashes gathered inside, but amid the odd shapes and shadows in the cabinet she couldn't make it out, and she had no desire to go shoving her hand inside without first knowing what she was looking at.

Turning to the wall behind her, she rummaged

in the mess of Grandpa Brown's coat and flicked the switch.

The very moment the hallway light came on, the lightbulb in the den shattered.

Shannon yelped, instinctively reaching up to cover her face as her eyes flitted up toward the bulb. In the purplish afterglow of the extinguished bulb she saw glittering streams of tiny, iridescent glass shards sprinkling out of the clenched fingers of a ratty, many-knuckled fist; then darkness overwhelmed the den and the hand was swallowed by shadow.

But not gone. She screamed as something scuttled toward her, louder, louder, louder above her head—

The fist lashed forward lightning-fast on its impossibly long arm and punched through the bulb right above her head. The deafening sound of smashed glass just inches from her skull was followed by a hail of tiny, sharp pieces all around her and she ducked, covering her head with both hands.

Staggering into the den away from the dreadful creature above her head, Shannon moaned as glass crunched beneath her feet, almost slamming into the coffee table all over again. "Leave me alone!" she yelled. "Fucking leave me alone!"

The thing scuttled away behind her. Her eyes shot up – just as an explosion of greasy yellow light blasted the window across from her. The L was coming around again, the monorail shuddering and the building rattling with it. The rails flashed and flickered in every shade of neon, illuminated by the ever-growing lamps of the oncoming locomotive and the pulsing waves of light from the street below…

Time stopped.

He stood on the rails facing the train, a pale-faced bony shadow in the wind. Lances of rain flashed around him but he didn't wobble, didn't move. His arms hung by his sides, bone-white hands smashed by the barnacle-like cones of all the knuckles that shouldn't be there. His eyes shone like two white discs in the skeletal mess of his face, his skin thin and translucent, his hair a matted white shock.

The next second passed by like an eternity stretched out to the power of a number she'd never be able to count to in her lifetime; moments later, she would realise that no time at all had passed, but in this silent, terrible fragment of time she was frozen, the world around her moving incomprehensibly, glacially slow.

Grandpa Brown turned his head toward her so slowly that she could almost hear the creak of bone on bone. His eyes flashed bright pink, then terrible emerald green, in the neon glow of a bodega's throbbing sign beneath the monorail.

The train hit him.

It appeared out of nowhere, smashing into the world framed by the window like a bullet into bone. The second its shining metal nose touched Grandpa Brown's flickering, ghostly silhouette he exploded into a cloud of thick, red clots, the mist of his body disappearing immediately in the rain – but she could still see him, his bones forced out of his carcass, his arms and legs stretching, extending, becoming impossible, peeling snakes of flesh as the train burrowed through him.

The light in the train's cabin blinked out.

Shannon's breath hitched in her throat as the train passed the window, lights going out one by one. Every tiny window along the body of the carriage blinked out, yellow to hell-black, one by one by one by one by one as Grandpa Brown's awful spirit passed through it—

She heard the grinding of metal on metal and an awful shriek of brakes, screams of panic as every carriage exploded into pitch-black chaos. And then an impossibly loud, long, shuddering groan as the train shot off the rails and keened out of the sky, plummeting toward the rain-slicked street below.

Shannon screamed as the L ploughed into concrete and crumpled far beneath her, and only then did she realise that she'd been watching all of this through a thick, glossy film of Grandpa Brown's blood on the windowpane.

<u>A NOTE FROM THE AUTHOR</u>

Thank you for reading *Dead Engines*. As an independent author every single person reading my work is so valued and I can't express how much your time means to me. For more of my books, follow me on Instagram @heath_horrorwriter or check out my website derekheathhorror.com where I'll keep you updated on future releases.

I hope you enjoyed! If so, please leave a review on Amazon if you can. I'd love to know what you thought.

<u>ALSO AVAILABLE FROM THE AUTHOR</u>

Day of the Mummy
Night of the Bunny
Dark Nights (Stories)
Moondisc
Empire of Cold
Endless Living Organ Massacre
Drop Bear (Outback Terror: Book One)
Parliament of Witches
Burrow

www.ingramcontent.com/pod-product-compliance
Lightning Source LLC
Chambersburg PA
CBHW031248210726

48287CB00003B/949